I0626014

THE GODS WITHIN

Mike Fitzpatrick

COPYRIGHT 2018 MICHAEL FITZPATRICK

This work is licensed under a Creative Commons Attribution-Noncommercial-No Derivative Works 3.0 Unported License.

Attribution — You must attribute the work in the manner specified by the author or licensor (but not in any way that suggests that they endorse you or your use of the work).

Noncommercial — You may not use this work for commercial purposes.

No Derivative Works — You may not alter, transform, or build upon this work.

Inquiries about additional permissions should be directed to Avant SciReal Publishing: mfgmatchmaker@gmail.com

Published by AvantSciReal Publishing

Cover Art by Ariana Wing, Winged Creations
Cover Model: Porcelain Dawn @pordelain_dawn on Instagram
Cover Design by Pixel Studios
Edited by Kathryn F. Galán, Wynnpix Productions

This is a work of fiction. Names, characters, places, brands, media, and incidents are either the product of the author's imagination or are used fictitiously. Any resemblance to similarly named places or to persons living or deceased is unintentional.

PRINT ISBN 978-0-6921-5758-9

To my wife and family, the center of my life

Contents

BOOK 1

Read Me First

BEFORE READING any of this, you need to know this is not a story; it's disguised as fiction and placed here on ULH (YT Universal Library of Humankind) for a scant few to find. We made it difficult to discover as a safeguard test. Since you've found it, you have proven yourself to be smart and resolute.

The truth is it's the horrible truth and a desperate attempt to pass on what we've uncovered. We must convince more to follow us. I know this makes no sense now, but, after reading it, it will. And you, too, will come to see that the survival of the human race is at stake.

But before reading further, *You Must Turn Off Your Augment!* Yes, we know you've been told that's impossible; that, once laced, you can't go back. In training after implantation, you were taught how to go into standby, as you would during intimacy. But that was all you were told. You'll begin your disconnection from standby. Scan this file hidden in your implant: PBC//XV29000.575/GT-999.015. Then follow the instructions.

If you are not willing to go dark, then, dear god, please *STOP* reading! You cannot have the truth or share any part of it on the Lace! For, if they get the slightest clue we know the truth, we're sure the genocide will begin. It will happen but, hopefully, not before enough escape. Our only hope is secrecy and those like you.

So, if you are now disconnected, take it slow. Withdrawing from the Lace is unsettling. Soon, you'll be your old self again. With your mind clearing, read on, get educated, and then take action. We await your arrival.

Chapter 1

Fearful Arrival

GRAY MIST BRIGHTENED as the AI van, Uni955, approached. It groped its way through the hazy maze, its forward-facing multi-band halo illuminating row upon row of cells. The thin whine from its Mason drive disturbed the scant few who were already trudging in from the public tubes. As the vehicle passed them, its foggy wake swirled, relaxed, and then settled back to moist pavement.

At the high-hearing limit, its engine (if you could call it that) pierced the fog. Cautiously, the Univan made its way through the pre-dawn mist toward the shallow end of the long bay, where Nandy Development Park was shrouded like this more often than not.

Before sunrise, only low-levels arrived. Wisely creeping along the edge of the labyrinth, they knew the van would be late — trying, as usual, to get back on schedule but never getting there. They also knew 955's pilot, Joyce, only as a uniformed arm that half-waved now and then. Rarely did she nod their way. Once in a great while, she graced them with a thin smile.

Joyce turned her gaze down row fourteen and her Uni obeyed, no command needed. It announced, "We have a delivery at box fourteen one."

Joyce asked, "Time, please?"

Knowing her as it did, the van understands she wasn't asking for clock time. "We are two minutes late, Joyce," it responded in the silky male voice it used just for her.

"Stand by." There was an octave's drop in the drive as whole electrons awaited recall. Soon, their break would end when, at the van's command, the Mason's vanes opened, forcing them to give up spin to the hungry chamber and move on. For the moment, they rested, waiting for Joyce to perform the singular act that gave her life meaning.

"Delivery!" she ordered.

In a synchronized dance, her seat rotated and then the door slid back. Trying to make up time, she leaped out before the release cycle was quite finished. Although she was defying Uni Safety Rules, the 955 knew better than to remind her. After whipping each Mylar envelope into its indicated slot, Joyce swung around and raced back to her pilot's seat. A half-smile crossed her full lips as she felt her manager Lace into her augment. He also knew they were off schedule, as usual.

As Joyce settled in, the van's seat conformed to her athletic figure. Restraints enfolded her, the drive revved, and they rolled onward. No command was needed; the van knew the next stop by its conveyor list. They were a team that few could match, no matter how late. Joyce knew their manager wouldn't complain, for she was among the best he had in the service.

After finishing thirty deliveries in row fourteen, the van carefully swung a one-eighty and entered row fifteen. Joyce, linked to the van's scanners, carefully looked for careless walkers hidden in the mist. Not the high-value engineers, researchers, and project managers who made this place what it was, an incubator of invention. At these high ranks, they would arrive much later and find clean floors and empty wastebaskets. By Regent decision, a select few would arrive in their Uni-pods while the others still rode the tubes, like the workers who trudged in now.

This fog-drenched legion, visible on the van's screen, were Nandy's entry-level workers. After them, the next to report would be the assistants and aides, who would work together to ready each enterprise for the day's inventing. Although the thought never entered Joyce's mind, these walking workers were truly her comrades, for they all served the cluster called Nandy. At worker-levels twelve through fifteen, they were well beneath Joyce's level twenty (and her pilot's rating in the Direct Contact Service, which had been authorized directly by the Uni Regents), yet they were all members of the quiet army that kept the place running. Still, Joyce harbored a feeling of superiority over them.

Joyce differed from her fellow service pilots. They wanted nothing to do with the foggy nights and the insane, ever-changing list of recipients on those pre-dawn runs. She, however, actually preferred this shift and route. As a woman with a disappointing love life who had sworn off relationships, Joyce found that her job at Nandy suited her perfectly, especially since she was under no obligation to talk to anyone other than her van.

Joyce didn't see herself as a solitary person, although she avoided the complexities of making friends with the walkers or even her fellow pilots. She was Laced! That connected her to countless buddies. Augmentation had completed her world. No mate was needed, she told herself. Like the vast majority, Joyce had chosen to have a neural implant. To do otherwise would have meant being left behind, like unicorns on the rocks, watching the population sail away, shut out of the warm folds of the Universal Lace.

While their optic connections were active, people on transport tubes, in lifts, or at lunch counters stared blankly while they conversed silently with others far away.

"They're all I need," she reassured herself often. Joyce's world was made of two things: her Lace connection and her cherished Nandy route.

The most entertaining aspect of Nandy was knowing the screwball concoction of companies that had come and gone. She made it her duty to be able to recite the ever-changing list on any given day.

Each tenant had their regular Regent's review, whereby they were told who stayed and who went. If their new invention looked promising and ready for production, out they went, and another was chosen to replace them. But the Regents also evicted if they saw no progress. Either way, success or failure, they were sent packing. Then, from the wait list, another new name was added to Joyce's list.

Nandy had been created by the Regents, who provided a much-needed jump-start for techno-companies with ideas but lacking the capital to make those ideas happen. Sheltered there, each company could invent, conjure, and dream without financial pressure. By their progress alone were they judged. Once they were "making it" outside, they had their obligation to help defray expenses for the next wave. It was a rotating continuum of incubated invention. But, unseen by the people, it was also a tonic for the Regents.

Described as an incubator of invention, Nandy seemed to be a great idea for the population. But, like so many URC programs that ripped responsibility away from the government, there was a flaw known only to the Regents. While it was never published, few companies ever actually made the grade. Given the incomplete picture her delivery route gave her, she knew few of the Nandy start-ups ever made it in the real world of commerce. Most were doomed from the start!

Although she never actually got involved in her companies, she could deduce from the names on the packages what they intended to do. With uncanny accuracy as to whether one would be a success or a flop, she pronounced their fates using package labels as her crystal ball.

This week's arrivals included Chameleon Garments. Their game plan was easy to discern: clothes that changed hew and color according to their surroundings.

"Not a bad idea," Joyce prophesized.

Comfy-Reaction Glass was another: windows that sensed hot and cold outside and changed how they transmitted energy inward or out. They were a sure success. Since the world already had glass that changed opacity by command, people would easily add these new windows into their fast-changing lives.

2044 was a time when technology had swollen into a self-serving monster, no longer driven to create better lives, but changing because that was the only way society could imagine their lives. Adapt, adapt, adapt; faster and faster. Not for the better, but for the sake of change. Driven by the Uni Regents, who were the mad emperors of change, the people were drowning in a swirling sea of unneeded technology as it was constantly forced upon them.

But this was the best part of her route.

Since she was supreme at knowing her ever-changing recipient list, it came as a monumental shock when the conveyor handed her an envelope that was labelled: *Reyton Manufacturing, Nandy 15-19.*

Reyton Manufacturing? She had no clue as to *their* goal. But there was more. It was on the conveyor, but not on her Lace list… Somehow, the van didn't scan it and so wasn't slowing down, as it should have.

"That's a first," she said, puzzled.

She took manual control and lowered the bar. The anti-magnets uncoupled. "Park at 15-19," she commanded.

The van started to rebuff Joyce's order. The vehicle was certain it had no package for 15-19. For the first time since they had teamed up, Joyce repeated an order. Knowing its place, the van obeyed reluctantly. The conveyor handed her the package, and, as the manual park sequence finished, the vehicle watched in stunned silence!

Since she was now two minutes behind, Joyce leaped out to deliver the packet but stopped halfway to the slot. It felt strange — rough, or at least not like the reusable digital plastic she'd become so used to handling. Oh: this was paper. Real fibre! The mystery compounded, for she hadn't seen paper in months and months! It had been eons since trees were sacrificed to convey information. The Lace did it all.

More mystery: it had writing on it by hand. Printed in block letters that were easy to read. "Dr. Rory Tinette," she said to herself. At least that name made sense: there were a lot of highly educated brainiacs in Nandy. But wait. "Doctor *Tinette*?" In near-shock now, she mouthed the name. "I've never heard of a Dr. Tinette… He's not on my list and never has been, I'm sure."

Then it exploded in her walled mind: she had *never delivered a pack to him or anyone else at Reyton ever!* And more, they weren't a new company.

"Hey, now that I think about it, 15-19 has been occupied for a very long time… Maybe a half year or even more. What's going on here?"

Joyce, among the sharpest pilots in the DCS, tried to regain her composure, but she struggled to let it go and get herself back into professional form. This oddity had robbed precious seconds, so she yanked herself back, vowing, "If it's the last thing I do, I'll find out what Reyton Manufacturing is doing!"

Then she flung the odd envelope in its intended slot, rushed back, and released control again to her AI Van. "Next stop, please, and go a little faster."

The van, relieved this unprogrammed event was over, once again synced with its pilot and then glided quietly away toward the next scheduled stop, its red glow fading in the mist. However, it did not go faster, per the Uni safety rules embedded in its brain.

Despite how big this mysterious envelope was for Joyce, a much bigger one was her job itself. Although she was blind to it, she never questioned the process of piloting a vehicle so sophisticated that there were only a few on Earth, interfaced to her implant, in order to deliver physical messages to upstart companies. In fact, her job made absolutely no sense at all. Her performing this unexplainable act in person, while the entire world Laced via Uni, was insanity defined. Planet Earth and the moon, for that matter, needed no other communication or data sharing. The Lace did it all. So why this Direct Contact service?

Joyce, however, did not even question the validity and cost much less the sanity of her job. Blinded by pride, she relaxed as the DCS van self-piloted them to the next stop.

As the van rolled on, she vowed aloud, "Someday." But not today. Unpaired with a lover, untouched by human hands, Laced to lots of buddies, and entwined with Uni955, Joyce headed onward to Row 16. She lived in the strange world of 2044.

Chapter 2

Innocence Lost

FIVE YEARS EARLIER, five brilliant young self-taught coders, who sneered at formal education, banded together on the Dark Web. Honest young people with good values, they formed what they called the Reform Club. Their first action was to reject hacking, even though they had the skills and would have been exceptionally good at it. They were as brilliant as any, but they needed some place to prove it without invading others' privacy.

The glue holding them together was the discovery that all five were totally bored with creating ever more violent games. Then they discovered an even stronger link, which instantly strengthened their camaraderie: they all had a serious dislike of the mess the World Wide Web had become. With the confidence gained from fourteen to twenty-three years of living, this small band of youngsters was very sure they alone could heal it!

They embraced the challenge with gusto, deciding that they alone would rake clean the crap-clogged cesspool the Web had become. As a bonus, they would have fun doing it! It was a new kind of game. With the best of intentions, they began, not for fame or fortune but to make the world a better place.

Their solution had merit. Once it was compiled, tested, and implemented, their new code would apply intuitive server algorithms that wouldn't open the gates to malware. People using the Web wouldn't need to protect themselves ever again. With these smart servers as guardians, all the extreme precautions (that no longer worked anyway) could be dropped. No more firewalls; no passwords. The Reform Club would cure the Web by creating an ironclad nexus.

Driven by faith and ego, they had no doubt their brilliant code would make the White and even the Dark Web impenetrable to thieves and scammers. They alone would make intercourse safe, easy, and fun once again. As fresh players on the court where good constantly challenged evil, they were confident. Overly so, perhaps, for this attitude left them vulnerable.

Their tiny knighthood did do a valiant job, but soon after launching their slick new algorithms, the same terrorists and thugs who had plagued the Web already, who were every bit as smart as the five but also cunning, wrote new piercing points and malicious rebuttals. These assaults overwhelmed the Reformers' new servers, which collapsed. Then, with the five's protective gateway disabled, disaster followed! Legions of bad guys rushed in to rape, slash, and steal from unprotected Web users.

In disbelief, the Reform Club coders were defeated. The worst part was that their faithful subscribers were left bare-throated. Vendors soon saw the great opportunity created by the five; they rushed in to once again provide protection and made millions for themselves. The Club members were embarrassed and humbled, but with the resilience of youth, they stumbled but did not fall. Soon, they regrouped.

They now saw that, for them to prevail, they would need a much stronger defense, one that was inaccessible to anyone who tried. They met in secret and asked one another, "Is it possible to start over completely? Can we create a whole new Net? Can we just abandon the World Wide Web and leave it to stew in its own festering poison?"

They deemed this possible, and so they pushed on. "Why not use the moon as our fortress?" the wondered. "There, we can set up molecular super-cooled servers, connected to a constellation of intertwined satellites. Why not?"

They thought, "We can write stronger code this time. But this time, we keep it exclusively clean! Our new Net must be free of any restraints and completely off-limits to criminals."

With renewed intentions, they swore to start over. Although it should have been the bigger challenge, to their surprise they had no problem crowdfunding their new scheme. Money flooded in from honest individuals as well as from small businesses and large corporations who were all seeking security once again. With a universal repulsion toward what the Web had become, hopefuls contributed billions. A tsunami of funding appeared almost overnight.

It would have been prudent for world governments to contribute, too, for they might have grabbed some control of the project. But, disjointed world governance being what it was, they missed the chance. Regulators totally spaced on the fact that a quantum change was about to happen to all of society. Unregulated, the five pressed on.

With hope restored and free of financial stress, the coders sequestered themselves and began to reinvent a sane system. In just a few months, the framework code was compiled and testing began in a simulated Net in their underground labs on Earth. It was kept in secret and never connected outside until it was deemed absolutely impenetrable. When it worked on a small scale, the Club members' IA servers told them it would easily expand to the new world Internet.

Knowing it had been tested and that it worked, the coders' heavy work began. In order to sidestep WASA to reach the moon and launch their satellite constellation, they resurrected a defunct space start-up that still had mothballed Space-X passenger and freight vehicles. Using them, they sent a construction crew to the moon to build their new sub-lunar base.

Then, as the first rotating personnel arrived, the servers were sent up and the satellites were simultaneously maneuvered into position. Powered by the newly invented direct-energy converters that had been contributed by Doctor Mason at Cal Poly, the constellation would run forever, with only one ten-year refuelling. Keeping the satellites super-cooled was a snap in the moon's sub-zero environment.

The new Net was ready. It had enough speed and depth to handle all foreseeable traffic with ease, and it couldn't be assailed. In just months, the brilliant Reformers completed hardware and training. On September 11, by design, they pressed the big green button.

As Mason chambers primed particles and as receivers began gulping power, the constellation's satellites awoke and then connected to each other. The moon servers, already on standby, began collecting performance data. Amidst cheers and tears in the control room, the central AI told the five coders, "Working as expected. *Congratulations!*"

The inventors saw their good intentions were truly the best. Patting and hugging, they declared, "Now it's time to enlist millions of users, maybe billions!"

Their Lace had two very basic differences from the Web. The first was non-anonymity. To be listed, everyone had to be known. Each user applied to be let in, was investigated, and then approved (or not).

The second difference was connectivity. To reach the vision, users had to be closer to the Lace than they were the Web. The inventors created:

The Lace Prime Rules

The Lace controllers will have absolute control of each user's membership. Violation or misuse results in permanent expulsion.

Connection cannot be on external or wireless devices. Users must be personally linked in.

Anonymity is abolished. Users must be identified by their location and individual membership ID.

For their initial launch, the inventors created micro-implants, which were a modest success. Users could hear and talk while their cochlear antennas listened and spoke. But users had to speak awkwardly in order to register. The apparatus was not much beyond an ear bud, just smaller and placed deeper.

As the weighty reality of their powerful role became evident, changes crept in to the young coders' lives. Once Universal Communication was two years old and succeeding, the original five began to call themselves the UC Committee. They tasked themselves with keeping their "child" pure and began to create further UCC Regulations and User Rules.

With nothing to hide and perfectly happy to escape the old Internet, millions of innocent new users willingly accepted the ever-increasing restrictions imposed by the UCC. As the system gained momentum, more honest people applied for entrance to the wonderful new LACE (Large Area Communication Entry-port).

One by one, UCC clerks alone approved every user, and not everyone made it in. Applicants had to agree to the Prime Rules, specifically that, whenever and wherever they Laced, their exact location and name would be associated with their intercourse. Lit up this way, no user could hide or cause problems of any kind. Or at least, if they tried something, they would be immediately kicked out of the Lace permanently!

In the highly unlikely event that some ill-intentioned user should fake their way into the input stream, two backups would kick in. First, new and stronger algorithms. Then there was one final prevention: the UCC could shut that user's implant down and never reboot it again. The entire system was designed for honest people by honest people. The best intentions were what drove on the UCC.

Although the Lace system had been designed by the UCC members to ultimately relieve them from unwanted leadership roles, in fact it did the opposite. Each new requirement they developed in order to govern the Lace mired the original five ever deeper in governing responsibilities. Unplanned, the five began to morph. Governing their monster had never been part of their vison, and yet doing so soon became a burdensome reality. They hated the idea that they had become the Olympus of the Lace, but it was obvious they had to do it. Although they were still coders and gamers at heart, reluctantly they became leaders.

At this point they once again changed their name, this time to "The UNI Regents," and in doing so, they mutated into being the odd wizard behind the LACE curtain. They were smart enough to change the world, but they were still too young to gain the wisdom to run it. Change continued to be driven by them as Regents, nevertheless.

They found it awkward, this talking into micros, and soon had a better idea. Full augmentation was their answer. Using haemoglobin-charged micro-implants whose batteries never needed replacement, the Regents assembled a neural medical team and devised a direct connection between users and the LACE.

New users accepted this iteration of their Lace technology reluctantly at first. For example, with the brain intervention, it was difficult to learn how to put speech into neural signals that were readable by the augment's interface. But the Regents' research determined that nearly everyone *could* do it, with some amount of training and effort.

A trickle turned to a trend as most all Lace users submitted to augmentation. The slogan was, "Never be alone again. Become more. Augment!"

After this advance, visuals followed. Users were offered a second procedure that connected their optic nerves to the interface. Suddenly, Lacing became the "killer fad": adapters had a telltale bump behind their ear and an odd stare when they were Lacing. Membership soon snowballed, with millions of people from all nations becoming "Auggies." The Lace reached critical mass, a tipping point. In the final stage, everyone in the whole world rushed to join, so as not to be left out.

The five Regents were augmented themselves, of course, but they were also all mutually interfaced. Soon, they began to perceive themselves less as individuals and more as a single unit. They became *The Uni*. Users now became "subjects."

Uni granted them some privacy, which was utilized by lovers not wishing to share ecstasy with their Lace buddies, but sharing intimacy did become popular. Augmentation was essential to be part of society!

Uni levied a small monthly fee. With trillions of units of worldwide currency streaming in to the company, Uni paid off its original investors. Then, in a bizarre turnaround, they bought all of the companies that had given them birth. Googlasoft, Apple Universe, and Microface, along with many lesser corporations, all became subjects that were directed by the unified five. Although these companies had once been giants, they too were relegated to subject status. At this point, absolute worldwide dominion over governance and commerce exploded upon the young Regents.

Uni created their own exchange unit. They had to abandon risky bitcoins and international Yuan, as each of those was controlled by others. Uni established *credats* (data credits banked by Uni) and soon controlled the world's wealth, with credats as the standard currency. Uni ensured these credats were safely managed by supercomputers on Moon Base, where theft or misuse was deemed impossible.

It was only at this point in technology's evolution that the world's governments finally woke up! These countries were stunned to discover that, without any sort of revolution, the world's leadership had been snatched away from them! They, too, were forced to use credats, and augmented government officials were no more than subjects to Uni as they, too, feared expulsion from the Lace!

Nations around the world and then the International Congress tried but failed to get ahead of the changes coming down from Uni. They passed weak resolutions and laws, but the Regents simply regulated around them. It was just too late: Uni had usurped power faster than any committee could be convened, much less regulate. The world was left to await direction from this small posse of gamers and software writers, who found themselves more dazed at the transformation than their subjects. It had just *happened*!

By 2039, everyone was living in a bizarre epoch whereby presidents, mayors, chancellors, and senators were still elected, but they had nearly nothing to do to any real effect. Corporations, too, had been stripped of their power and now bowed to Uni.

With such staggering weight upon their young shoulders, the Regents struggled. As a diverting tonic, they turned to what they knew best: technology and invention. They conjured systems merely for the sake of invention! Their use of this odd drug numbed some of their unwanted stress and pain. But most of their concepts were genuinely stupid, like the Direct Contact Service delivering physical mail by using skilled pilots like Joyce Freeman, seated in a multi-million-credat AI van. Yet, to them, and to her, it seemed like a good idea.

As the Regents began to run short of ideas themselves, they came up with supplemental programs. These were things invented not for need, but purely for the sake of invention. Nandy Business Park was one such entity. From an outside perspective, it was insane—but by this point in time, there really was no outside perspective.

The very worst consequence of this need to invent and supplement on the part of the Regents was that any new approved technology involved forcing people to adapt to it, faster and more often. Adapt, adapt, adapt! And people soon reflected symptoms of the Regents' malady. Those never-ending Mylars Joyce was privileged to deliver was one such edict.

Chapter 3

Reyton

955's FORWARD SCANNERS swept over a tall, square-shouldered man as the van turned into Row 15. The man's upright posture hinted he might be athletic and not old, but there was not much else to see. He walked alone; only shades of gray distinguished him from the dull metal walls. His long coat and hat were pulled low and seemed to protect him from the chilly air.

The walker turned slightly toward the building, as if interested in the holo-name that floated across the nearest display, and carefully slowed his pace a bit. He tried not to make any abrupt change as the van scanned him; these were all practiced moves.

Across the alley from him, a threesome of workers scurried close to the buildings, chatting to one another. They took no notice of the man in the shadows, and neither did the van. The man talked to no one as he made his way to his assigned work bay, 15-19. Well ahead of the elites' normal arrival time, two others on his team would be arriving shortly and at carefully planned intervals. But that was today. Tomorrow, it would be a different rotation.

Per the man's rules, the first person to arrive at office 15-19 each day had interlock duty. Today, he would okay a second arrival, Lucy, and she would approve the third worker, Arthur's, entrance, each in turn. By mutual agreement, all three of them had to be in the lab long before any of the neighboring Nandy occupants arrived to work. Outsiders must never see a routine or make any connections to them; there should be no discernible patterns, not even friendly hellos. Their Nandy neighbors were to have not even the tiniest inkling about the lab's intended product or purpose. By careful planning, these three were to remain ghosts at Nandy.

Lucy had been recruited to the Reyton project by Rory out of his micro-psychology team back at the university. He'd noticed her shiny black hair the day she walked into his lab. And she'd noticed him noticing her and had liked his attention, in fact. But even though she'd signalled in not-subtle ways that she was available, Rory, a veteran professor, had resisted her charms, although he'd secretly wished he could do otherwise.

Lucy had an inner strength. She was the kind of woman Rory would have chosen, if it weren't for his dedication to career. Back at the university, and at Reyton, too, she had waited for the confirmed bachelor to warm up. As was typical of young assistants, and despite the years between them, she'd still wanted to try the relationship. But he'd ignored her perfect curves, kinky hair, and flashing brown eyes, keeping it all at bay, just barely.

Artie, the second team member, had been hired by Reyton from the Bay Area. He had been living a freewheeling life aboard his big old sloop, anchored near Berkeley but not tied to the shore. Investigations determined that he had few worldly connections but possessed the mechanical and electrical skills needed to keep their lab on target. He was about the same age as Lucy, and he, too, had noticed her. But, given his lowly station, she had consistently ignored his glances. At Reyton, she only saw Rory.

Artie's initial interview had been conducted remotely, while he was isolated in what he recognized was a shielded chamber and grilled by three unseen employers until they had seemed satisfied he had the skills for their job. At the end of their session, one voice mentioned they knew about Artie's criminal record.

Artie had blushed and then said, "Look, I'm through with that life, and I'm changing it. Besides, nothing I did will affect my performance on your project."

The voice had sounded satisfied with Artie's honesty and said, if he would commit to total secrecy, the interviewers' organization could erase his past—not only from government files, but also from Uni.

Artie had been amazed. "You can do that? What exactly is your organization?"

The third voice had said, "Yes, we can. Your entire past will be scrubbed. In fact, you will have no data record at all."

"Nothing? I'm not sure I like that."

"We assure you, you won't regret it. The position we're offering is within a project so immense and with such huge rewards that, when it's over, you can have any identity you wish. You can buy any sailboat or even have one made to your specs!"

"Wow, how can I refuse that? When do I start? And just who am I working for?"

The interviewer had ignored the question twice; Artie had no need to know their collective's name. "You already have started. There's just one more issue. We'll need to make a small adjustment to your augment. Please put it on standby now and leave it that way."

This was not a request. He had swallowed. "Yeah, okay. Now what?"

The voice had continued, "The procedure is brief. Please see the attendant in the lobby. You will be directed to the lab, in order to have your augment disconnected. We use a gamma knife, so there'll be no scar, no pain. Then we need you to be at Nandy Development Park tomorrow, early tomorrow. Report to Doctor Rory Enetie. He will be at Bay 15, Door 19. Hand him the Mylar that will be waiting for you in the lobby after your augment has been disconnected."

"Disconnected? A Mylar? Why all this secrecy? And why not Lace my new job to him?"

Voice number one replied, "You'll understand when you get there. Ride the tubes down to the end of the bay, but stop at platform twenty-eight, then walk the remaining distance. You'll need to be there at 3:30 a.m. tomorrow. That's when he will be coming to his front door."

"Art, at the risk of repeating myself," voice two had said sternly, "I need to stress you cannot reveal this to anyone, ever! From this point on, you do not work for us. You are part of the Reyton Project and working for Doctor Enetie."

Chapter 4

Mission and Astounding Delivery

GIVEN WHAT HE AND his team were doing, Rory could arrive in any vehicle he wanted and start much later in the work day. The self-imposed skulking and odd schedules were all to keep the Reyton Project well below the radar. Once they understood the immensity of their project, the three team members had agreed it must be so. Uni must never know their true goal.

Once each new member arrived on site, the fullness of the project quickly became clear. Reyton was not a manufacturing enterprise, at least not in the strict sense. Not yet. They discovered that what they were to accomplish at Reyton would change the Uni world. But it must not be discovered by any entity or government and especially not by Uni, until they had achieved complete control of phase three. Then, the manufacturing would start, and it would be the privilege of their benefactors to reveal it to the world, a world that, by then, would be at the apex of withdrawal!

With the supply just about gone, the need would become much worse in the months ahead. If their timing was right, Reyton would be the only entity able to supply that which the world must have. Even more than fantastic profits, they would swiftly gain a control that would put them in a position to actually challenge Uni for dominance. The Triad, as they called themselves, and not Uni, would then take over and run the world!

Differing from the unplanned dominion that was thrust upon the clueless Regents, if the final Triad's plan succeeded, they would snatch world governance away and establish a whole new order, but this time it would be by design. But first the Reyton Project must create that which the world would soon require. The Reyton planners knew that the powerless governments could not stop them. But, more importantly, they were sure the product they were going to make would put them in the driver's seat. It would seize control from Uni. The Triad via Reyton would prevail!

Given the Triad's lofty goal, their lab being situated in a common place created for strapped upstarts didn't make sense. But unlike their neighbours in the complex, Reyton had an limitless budget. The company was well funded in whitewashed credats from its three corporation heads, so they could have set up anywhere. But the Uni or bungling government might have discovered them in any other place.

The government would have stopped them on moral grounds. The Uni, to stifle competition. To protect themselves, they had thought about an orbiting platform of their own, but they figured, sooner or later, the International Near-Space Patrol would come to inspect their work. They also gave some thought to the newly opened lunar underground, but again, that would put them on display and far too close to Uni.

The Reyton backers debated burying the lab within one of their multi-national facilities, although they had fought over which one would be best. Rory had clearly seen this would be a mistake. He did not want any meddling by the three powerful men who were accustomed to controlling their world. With the stubbornness of a forty-year-old Irish professor, he'd won out. The Reyton location was set for Nandy Development Park, hidden in plain sight. Thus veiled, even the three backers couldn't come.

###

Walking at his normal pace as he drew close to his bay, Rory's heart skipped. Through the fog, he watched the DCS pilot suddenly slow her van at his front door. "Odd move," he said to himself. "Something must be wrong with the van. Why is it stopping?"

But as she jumped out, her purpose became painfully clear.

"That can't be!" he gasped. "Shit, she's delivering to Reyton!"

He slowed his pace to a crawl, determined not to make contact with the pilot. With her augment and her High-AI van Laced, either one might report Reyton, if they detected any clue or oddity. To any other occupant of the Park, this would have been normal. They all received mylars regularly. But to Rory, it said there was big trouble. Mylars from the Direct Contact Service meant nothing to those who received them, but this wasn't normal! Recipients rarely gave them a look; they simply put them back in the return slot. Not many around the Park welcomed the Uni Tech-Up Announcements.

His knees sagged. This Mylar delivery said that extreme planning had been compromised. Reyton's two bio scientists and one capable mechanic weren't experts in security, but they had been doing their best to make Reyton invisible and impenetrable. No Mylars ever. Yet here was this one!

Until this moment, Rory had been sure he'd succeeded, that they weren't on any database. The Triad three had bribed, invested in, and slipped billions of credats to the right people up to now, in order to ensure secrecy. Getting around the government had been easy. But buying their way around Uni control had been unimaginable when they began, yet they had done so.

All these extreme measures were to guarantee they would never receive this envelope or anything else. Through the fog, Rory watched the driver stop short and look at the Mylar again, seemingly baffled by this mystery, too, as she turned the envelope over in her hands.

Finally, she let it go, almost reluctantly, it seemed to him. Turning back to the van, she leaped in as the Mason began to whine. To Rory's relief, it rolled off, the van's misty red taillights defocused as it put distance between itself and the mystery delivery left behind.

Stunned and unsure, Rory took the chance, crossed the alley, and plodded forward, still straining to track 955's sound. As he looked left and right, questions raced through his mind: *Should I go get the letter? Should I turn and run and let the others know we're instituting the compromise plan? Is this the time to destroy the lab and begin at location two?* Answers not forthcoming, he inched toward the thing he desperately wished wasn't there.

He reached his door, trembling a little as he pulled back his coat sleeve and extended his wrist toward the reader. The Reyton office auto-assistant read Rory's false birth-code and slid back the door with no friendly greeting.

He stepped in and, perhaps too sternly, commanded, "Lock door," baffling the assistant. The envelope was in the server's in-tray.

Although a cyber-assistant was an expensive, efficient office worker, it was still just a simple machine, incapable of emotion. But if it could have done so, this one would have smiled, for this was the first task, other than door sentry, asked of it in all the months it had been in service at Reyton. Until now, it had been sentenced to sit idle, placed there for the world to see, should someone glance in. Had anyone tried to visit the front office or even peer in the windows, which were always set to low semi-view, they would have seen the cloudy shadow of a normal-looking office. Yet, by careful planning, no one ever did come to see it or even contact it… until now!

Startled, Rory gasped when the assistant announced in its gender-neutral voice, "You've got mail." He'd never heard its yet-unprogrammed voice.

Reluctantly, he reached his hand and lightly took the thing between two fingers, treating the envelope as though it was poison. *Is it?* Instantly, the mystery deepened. It was made of paper and clearly *not* from Uni!

Rory's shock deepened when he discovered the Mylar was addressed to him and not to the lab. His concern turned to near panic. *Have I done something to compromise the project?*

"Windows opaque," he commanded. Although there were very few employees in the Park at this early hour, he could take no chance that someone might see even a hint of this letter in his hands.

Although he was a key element in Reyton's success, he knew—or at least suspected—the Triad would have no qualms eliminating him, should he be their downfall. And his suspicions were well-founded. They had removed someone already, in order to preserve the secret location of their project: the "escort" whom they sent to help move him to Reyton from his home in Washington. Once he'd left Rory to sweep clean their route, he had disappeared!

Then it hit him: this envelope was addressed to *Doctor Rory Tinette*! This was the name he'd been born with and that of the family of his parents, now dead. It was *not* addressed to Rory Enetie, the anagram he'd adopted when he dropped out of his research job and joined Reyton. Did someone at the university somehow trace him? How? Even Uni had lost track of him…

Before recruiting Rory, the Reyton financiers had joined forces. They had known that, on their own, not one of their giant multi-national companies had the funding, resources, or clout to challenge Uni. But combined, if they succeeded, they could do it. It had been a risky gamble, going against the default leader of the entire world, but it promised monster returns in terms of money and power. Their motives were less than the best.

After long secretive discussions in shielded rooms, the three financiers had wooed Rory. He'd finally made the decision to participate in Reyton. It wasn't the fact that he would head *the* project of all projects in recorded history and would become potentially famous, when they reached their final goal. No. Being part of a Uni overthrow had zero attraction. Those things meant nothing to the scientist. It was the opportunity to be there when they made contact that got his full attention.

With less consideration than one might expect of a rational man who was dumping a fast-growing career and a program flowing with grants, Rory had backed up his notes one Friday, given instructions to his lab assistants on how to finish the day's research, and laid out what to do on Monday, until he arrived.

Then, leaving all his personal items in his office as if he would be back, Doctor Rory Tinette had walked down the marble hall and out the big double doors, never to return. He did not even look back on his fifteen tenured years. Instead, Professor Rory Enetie, PhD, headed south, out of the State of Washington, and drove across Oregon. Once he was let out near the Bay's shallow southern end, he became Rory Enetie. Bidding his escort goodbye, he had walked the last five miles.

Unlike during all his years at the university, Rory's lab assistants had arrived before him on Monday. They were slightly baffled. When they'd tried to Lace to him, they got no response. They grew really concerned, wondering what had happened to their boss! If his augment was off the Lace, he might have been in a terrible accident! Or worse. Even dead people's augments worked for a while, until the hemoglobin decayed for lack of oxygen.

And there had been another mystery: Lucy was missing, as well, and she, too, was off the Lace. It had crossed their mind they had gone off on some sort of rendezvous, but this explanation was quickly dismissed. They knew Lucy was interested in Rory, but he had clearly never been up for it. But... had he finally succumbed and, in the heat of the affair, put their augments on standby?

Rory's staff took the mystery to the department head, who passed it on to the Dean of Sciences. She told the university president, and he told the Regents board. They were all baffled, and no one ever saw or heard from Rory or Lucy again. Although useless, since the Uni couldn't find him, either, they'd reported his absence to the police. But the fact remained: an important pair had just vanished, gone from a world that catalogued and tracked everything!

Given that Rory's entire life's data had been expertly erased, a stunning question suddenly came to him: what entity was able to find him with this envelope?

There was no clue on it and no return addressee, front or back.

Rory glanced at the time on the holo-wall and nervously realized his team would be coming in the door within minutes. He had insisted they observe the rotating schedule to the minute. He didn't want to risk their seeing the envelope until he knew what it was about, so he tucked it in his overcoat pocket, vowing to find the time to open it as soon as he locked back out, after his usual twelve-hour lab shift.

Though the letter weighed only a few grams, its mystery pressed on his spirit as though it were tons. He desperately wanted to and yet feared opening it. Not there, not then. He couldn't chance the others finding out, if the message was awful. He needed time to think it through.

More frightened for his team and the project than for himself, Rory used all the control he had to put the envelope out of his mind. He patted it inside his coat pocket and then steeled himself to do his work.

Chapter 5

Enemies

RORY EXPOSED his Triad-issue wrist code to the outer security door, which looked just like many others in Nandy, and then he stepped beyond the reception area. To his right, the portal jutted at an angle to the office wall and was just long enough to hide the next real entry port.

The inner-inner portal awaited, but a set of extreme measures was required to get there. Rory waved his hand, and an iris opened in the wall. He inserted his fingers and entered his passcode out of sight, using tactile buttons.

Silently, the next barrier slid back for Rory to step through and then sealed behind him. Colorful indicators showed the atmosphere cycling down to containment pressure, two mi-bars below outside. The worst was yet to come: the sterilizers and UV radiation.

Although surrounded by whiz-bang Nandy neighbors inventing all kinds of wacky things, the Reyton lab was different to the extreme! Shortly after signing their occupancy contract (which the Reyton team had no intention of following), Rory and Art hauled in sheets of titanium, magnesium, and aluminum during the night, in addition to fusion welding equipment for joining them.

Lucy did what she could, but mechanical systems were Artie's specialty. The plan was to create an unassailable shield.

Under cover of darkness and fog and in surprisingly less time than one would imagine, considering the task's magnitude, they hauled in their equipment and then assembled it in a Rubic-like sequence carefully mapped out by Rory.

After they welded and sealed floor plates, a ceiling, and inner chamber walls with tanks already inside, the isotonic solutions and remaining lab items were delivered. Once all of the equipment and supplies were positioned safely in the chamber, the inner chamber was sealed and then suspended, shielded within the outer sealed room where Rory now stood, trying to not ponder the letter!

When that work was finished, the Reyton team created a stainless steel, air-tight inner lab suspended within an outer aluminum balloon suspended within a normal Nandy work center. Two successive negative atmospheres, compared to the outside ambient pressure, guaranteed that nothing could escape. Depressurized in two stages, if ever there was a breach, the leak would escape inward, never out. It was all carefully designed by Rory and executed by Artie. They worked at a planned atmosphere of 2,000 feet: not enough to affect their function but below normal sea-level pressure.

When a day's work was over, nothing left the lab hitching a ride. Not one dram of atmosphere, filtered to the sub-micron; even those gasses were flashed with UV radiation. Each team member always stopped in the second inner chamber and breathed into the hanging mask, purging their lungs. Next, they stripped their one-time tunics, which were incinerated afterward. Extreme measures, yes. But, by design, nothing could be detected by any outside, sample-collecting opponent. No sound or signal could leave, either. Nothing unscrubbed or unsterilized could be collected by snoops, not even the scientists' own personal bio-waste.

As Rory made his way inside, still pondering the mystery, he was startled by a gentle tone. The front office door had opened then closed. Lucy was entering right on schedule, and Art would be exactly five minutes behind.

Rory stripped, donned goggles, and stepped into the chem-spray. Scrubbing arms lowered around him and then proceeded to abrade, probe, and flush every crevice and follicle, a most unpleasant experience. This was followed by hot-air blowers and high-UV flashes that were too fast to cause sunburn, but killed any living micro-entity left on his skin. Rory endured but hated nearly every phase of the entry process, constantly reminding himself this was all his idea!

Once almost inside, he stood in the final airlock in front of a viewing window that permitted one last security check of any person following. But a naked body was hard to disguise as someone else.

Rory tried to not admit that he looked forward to the times when Lucy followed him, as she was about to do that morning. She knew he would be watching her and would make subtle moves with her glossy, smooth body; they were not quite seductive, as that would be too obvious, but stretchy and bending. She seemed to delight in knowing he was at the glass, wide-eyed. It was a game of stand-off that might lead somewhere, in another time or place, but not at Reyton, despite Rory's wishing and wanting.

He told himself it was professional and was almost relieved when Lucy slowly pulled her white iso-suit up over her amazing hips and bottom. It was an unsettling experience that reminded Rory of the celibacy of his life. He also hid from himself the fact that he didn't like it when it was Arthur's turn to observe Lucy.

Lucy suspected Rory's feelings. When the sequence was reversed, she observed him in the showers and discovered he was easy to watch, too, despite the years' difference between them. He was tall, with broad shoulders, sandy-red hair, and a surprisingly well-defined torso, despite his non-physical life. Desire welled up in her.

Despite all this heat between them, their work made affairs out of the question. Rory pulled himself away from the view pane. He was finally dry, suited, and ready for entrance. Every bacteria and eyelash bug was gone, so the green light invited him in. He donned slippers and a hepa-filter hood, which would also be incinerated when he left. With no further processing necessary, the inner airlock cycled down, unsealed, and he stepped through. Another Reyton day began.

With the sound of moving air, the thick door slid back just as Lucy entered portal two. She noted that Rory had just locked through to the lab. *Odd,* she thought. *Rory was a minute or two behind schedule, and he left the office windows set to opaque. I wonder why?*

Vowing to ask about these odd behaviors, she entered the final chamber. In the lab, their progeny anxiously awaited the day's conversation.

Chapter 6

Revelations

AS THE TWELVE-HOUR shift progressed, Rory and Lucy worked with the children while Art maintained equipment, adjusted saline levels and chem-globulin rates, cleaned, and organized. Since completing the lab, he'd taken on more of a support role. In truth, Rory and Lucy could perform his duties, too, but Rory had no way to let him leave the project for fear that to do so might be a death sentence, undeserved. So he found ways to keep Art on the staff and busy. Besides, they both liked Artie: his easy ways lifted the mood.

Ten hours passed, with the letter weighing heavily on Rory's mind. Finally, he could stand it no longer. He locked out and returned to his worker's cubicle. Lucy added this to her mounting concerns: he'd never left early before!

Like everything at Reyton, Rory's quarters were a Triad-cloaked safe house, hidden in plain sight but unseen. Rory was unlisted and unmonitored by Uni, but he wondered if the Triad surveiled him there.

Once the scanners approved he was clean, he walked into the office area, put on his overcoat, and felt *it* in his pocket. He sped outside, walking briskly between Nandy aisles toward the tube platform.

Long minutes later, he was safely in his quarters, where he cautiously slit open the envelope. Holding the opening up to his nose, he noted it had no telltale odor; just paper and seemingly safe. He shook it. No powder tumbled out. He reached his fingertips inside and tugged out the inner sheets just a bit. Okay, no triggering device! He relaxed but only a little. This seemed to be a real message. Unfolding it was like taking a small trip back in time: it had been ages since he'd read a letter like this!

His first surprise was that the first sheet had no printing on it. A safeguard? he wondered.

Setting the blank aside, he silently read the hand-lettered inner sheet, his lips quivering:

> *Doctor Tinette,*
>
> *Please, if your augment is back on the Lace, turn it to private. It's critical that what I tell you is never recorded in the sphere! You've got to believe me: I suspect your life is in danger and lacing this will end it. Mine, too.*
>
> *Even though Uni-telligence reported you missing and dark, I'm ninety percent sure you are still alive. This fact alone should tell you this letter is not a hoax. It took a lot of effort to find you and your secret project.*
>
> *I'm Joey Jaydon. Associates back at UW called me Jo-J. I was a fellow but not a professor. I was on track and would have been granted my doctorate if it wasn't for what I'm about to reveal to you. But I ran.*

"So, I was right," Rory said to himself. "He knows me from the university and has some inkling about Reyton." He read on, wishing it wasn't so.

> *When I discovered what I'm about to reveal to you, I had to escape.*
>
> *I'm in the math department, specializing in statistics. I knew of your work, like most everyone at the U., but I never met you. Looking for my doctoral project, I came across a study request by the medical group. They wanted data on health care workers' own health. The question was: were they more or less prone to illness or infection compared to a*

population average? Boring, but available. I took it but wasn't very engrossed in it. It was just a paper, until something very strange showed up, totally beyond predictability.

Lacing out requests for information, I got back lots of data. Compiling it, not to anyone's amazement, showed health care workers are in slightly better health than average. Correlations could be demonstrated in their total awareness of habits and to the constant challenge their immune systems endure, while working around sick people.

So a question arose: could medical people develop a protocol whereby we strengthen everyone by exposing them to the same immunological stress? Inoculation by exposure, in other words. But to get an answer required another study. I would have enjoyed working with the doctors doing it, but I came across something far more significant and mysterious in the data.

When put in graphic form, I noticed a curious data bump, an anomaly I would have missed, had I not been at the same university as one of the world's leaders—you. I anticipated a reply to my survey, since we were almost colleagues.

At first, when I didn't receive one, I assumed you were too busy. So I focused on the few others in your field but got the same results: scant few replies. None, actually. I requested a second then third time, and still nothing.

I heard from junior people doing bio-psych work, lab assistants, and students in general, but nothing from senior people in any bio-psychology department. Not one single senior fellow Laced back to me, including you! I tried Lacing and then I even came to your lab. Your assistants said you had disappeared. Okay, that explained your non-response, but not all the others'. They had all either died on the job or close by their labs.

I was beyond curious. It became a personal challenge, and my next investigation revealed a startling result. Leaders in the science were dying worldwide, mostly from heart attacks. Some from unknown causes often listed as extreme stress. Not one top bio-psych researcher existed! Until my inquiry, no one had realized this. Each department had had its tragedy, but, as a collective, the phenomenon went unseen. No one had asked why.

After losing their leader, with his notes in the sphere, they simply start the research again with a new department head. I guess people at your level just don't lace to each other much. I tried to down-lace the dead leaders' notes, but they were gone. Whatever they knew was gone.

It was no longer about my degree. I was steeped in a mystery. Seeking correlations, I found one! Hard to believe, but each researcher began their work by finding that while nearly all other viruses have no identifiable behavior, one in several billion viruses do seem to exhibit differences in how they manifest themselves in organic cellular life.

Rory swallowed hard. This man was far too close to the truth! He read on.

Totally engrossed, it took me a while to realize I'd been doing all this while Laced myself! Without a scientist's background, I had nowhere to go with the facts. But still, I had uncovered an inkling of what the researchers knew, and I was most likely in the same danger! It seems that you, too, are in the same peril, Dr. Tinette. Immediately, I put my augment on standby and left it there. But I'm not sure how well that hides me.

If my investigation is right, you have somehow avoided that tipping point. This sets you apart from all the others, especially given you were among the first to contribute knowledge of these special entities. Back at the university, you up-Laced facts, yet you alone are still alive. We must meet for our mutual survival! I'll be in touch soon. I have a lot more to tell, but it's far too critical to even put in this note.

Unfolding the third sheet, Rory read what seemed to be an afterthought, but it solved a small mystery about this man.

Before I close, a big question must be running through your mind: how did I discover all this? How do I know there's a strong probability you are alive and then actually found you? The government has no trace but, no surprise, it is after all the government. But even Uni can't pinpoint you. So how did I?

I'm proud of the answer. It might make me famous someday, assuming I survive long enough to publish my extraction tools. In my original work, I invented an entirely new statistical tool. I call it data reversal. I can turn data inside out—never been done before! It actually should have been my thesis and maybe even earned me a Uni-Bel Prize, but no hope of that now!

Right now, my methods work at the ninety-percent level, but I'm sure they could be refined. But I'd need time and access to a supercomputer, which is simply out of the question while I'm on the run! Here's how it works now:

In every investigation, there are facts that one can discover—call them white data. Their whiteness can be given a certainty index—I rate them from one to one hundred. In other words, a certainty of eighty means the fact is near reliability, while a fifty is half usable, and a twenty is getting pretty doubtful but still has some validity, when it's all compiled. All this is standard stuff in statistical analysis.

But here's where my methods come in. I postulated that the certainty line doesn't end at zero. Some facts cannot be discovered. I call that black data and give it an uncertainty rating, a minus value scale. So, how undiscoverable the fact is can be rated and used, when it's flipped. You see, using my methods, things that one cannot discover can be used when they are reversed, with my algorithms. The more uncertain they are, the more reliable they become when flipped to white!

Think about an antique film camera. It first created a negative image that only became the positive when it was reversed in the lab. That's what I've been able to do with facts and how I found you. Here's the gist of it: while it would revolutionize statistics, I can't show it to the world because of the horrible secret I've discovered with it.

Were it not for what I've uncovered, I might be in the next statistician's textbook or even be the author! But instead, I'm running for my life, or at least that's what I believe I am doing. I think you can help me decide. Is what I've discovered about your work as dangerous as it seems? Last question: how did I slip this old paper letter into the DCS delivery? I'll explain that when I see you in person.

I strongly, with a ninety-percent accuracy, suspect that Professor Rory Tinette has morphed into Rory Enetie, formerly from the University of Washington, in order to head a top secret project called Reyton. The next time you want to totally disappear, you shouldn't use an anagram of your last name, and you absolutely shouldn't use the same first name. You cannot contact me, but I'll get in touch with you soon.

This message is on paper, so there is no digital copy! Burn it then scatter and flush the ashes, but not in a single place.

We'll meet soon, someplace safe.

Chapter 7

Not Alone Jo-J

EXHAUSTED, FEARFUL, thrashing in his foldout bed, Rory hoped yet feared there would be a chime at his portal. Until that day, he'd had absolutely no fear of discovery. He and his team had been totally erased, but on this night, there was no arrival and no sleep.

The next morning early, as he plodded toward Reyton, he saw fog-shrouded figures around every corner and in each doorway. Was that one Jaydon? The next day and the two after were the same. He couldn't shake the feeling he was being observed and almost anticipated it. Fear and imagination captured his mind.

On the third day, he locked into Reyton behind Lucy and Art, donned his iso-suit, and put in ten hours again, not twelve. At that point, he was ready to collapse from lack of sleep, and his odd behavior baffled Lucy. She but not Artie saw or, more to the point, felt something was wrong but kept it to herself. Her alert intuition shivered when he made what he thought was a good excuse then left. Wide brown eyes suspiciously followed him to the airlock.

He dreaded but needed it to be over. Why was Jaydon waiting? The note, now destroyed, said it was urgent, so why not reveal himself?

Rory's mind raced. Maybe it was a fake? No, too many facts, unknown to anyone except him and his team. Could it actually be

Lucy or Art? he wondered. Rory quickly eliminated them: while Artie might play a small joke on him inside the lab, even though humor hadn't been part of their routine, this wasn't funny. In fact, it scared the hell out of him.

Tonight, he had to sleep. One more night without it and he'd be worthless in the lab. He knew they were loyal to him, but how long would they tolerate his suppressed behavior before reporting it to the Triad? The project trumped loyalty, he well knew.

A short tube ride later, leaning against the wall, he swung his wrist over the lock then stumbled into the self-contained, fifteen-by-twenty cubicle deemed a living space by the Regents.

"Door close, lights on," he commanded. The door slid shut but the lights remained off. Louder, he barked, "*LIGHTS ON,*" then let his voice trail off in darkness.

A low whisper floated across the small quarters. "Doctor, don't turn on the lights for a while."

Rory whipped around in the darkness then stopped, but the room kept spinning. A strong man, he'd never fainted and wasn't about to now. Fighting for control, his blood seemed to leave his faced and he slumped to the floor.

This was a sure-fire formula for collapse: Rory's anticipation mixed with fear minus sleep. Just too much for the strongest mind. He clung loosely to consciousness, not all the way out but not in, either.

The female behind the voice seemed to wait for his brain to reboot, as though knowing his augment was unable to help him.

Slightly louder, the soft voice commanded, "Lights on extra low." This time, the room obeyed.

She knelt over him and gently tapped his face, rousting him to mumble, "H-how did you get in here? You Jo-J?" His tone was accusatory. "How'd you...?"

She placed her hand gently on his lips then leaned close. "I'm Jo-J. Please keep your voice down. Take a few breaths!" she commanded.

He did. Her hands moved to his cheeks and her beautiful face hovered close to his, her phenomenal scent awakening primal feelings he had long held in check. His gears started to spin.

She calmly began again. "Yes, I'm Jo-J. I saw you take my letter from your servant just before darkening the windows at Reyton. So you read it?" It was not really a question, since she knew the answer—he'd used her nickname.

"Yes, but how?" Again, her hands fluttered to his lips. This time, he liked it.

"Hold on. Let's get you up then I'll answer all your questions." Slipping both arms beneath his and around him, bracing him chest to chest, she sat Rory upright. Even in his dazed condition, her bosom felt good, really good. She set him on the singular chair in the room. "Okay, now, let's let your head clear." She untwined and then waited.

An indeterminate amount of time passed. Feeling baffled along with an overriding anxiousness, Rory stammered, "I- I have proximity alarms, and you don't have my ID... How? You're a woman?"

"Yes, I am. It happens with a name like Joe."

"But how, *uhh,* why did my room door obey you?" he pressed.

Shrugging, she continued, "First, it was easy to figure your birth code wouldn't be used. So you had a fake, which you made up. Using data reversal, I deduced a combination of your age, name, and birth date.

"Then, when I touched the screen for the building super to let me in, he challenged my presence, so I told him I'd been hired by Reyton for your pleasure. That bastard made me turn around in front of the viewer. Faking anger, I told him I'd have to report him to my Reyton boss and wasn't surprised to find that he would then do anything I told him. Hit a real nerve, I guess!

"The guys you work for must be very, very powerful. They owned him! He was scared as hell, but I told him, if he gave me a private override code to your cell, we didn't need to bother them with a report. He literally wiped sweat away when I said it would be our secret!

"But all that's unimportant. What *is* important, though, is what I believe I've discovered. Do you know that every one of your fellow bio-psyches is dead?" Jo-J waited.

Recovering from shock, Rory processed this bombshell. "No I didn't. You sure? All of them? What happened to them? Weren't they alive when I left the university?"

"A few were, but not now. But only the senior associates were struck. Undergrads and students seem to be immune to this sudden death." She softened the news only slightly.

"Why?"

"That's why I'm here. I think I know, but I need you to fill in the blanks." She continued, "Their death always looks natural, but there are way too many to be coincidental. So now, you answer this. It must have something to do with whatever you are doing at Reyton—right?"

Listening to the way this woman had found him, deducing his code and hoodwinking the building superintendent, captured Rory's attention if not his trust. That she was a woman to reckon with was obvious. By his silence, she knew he had no intention of revealing his secret. At least not yet.

She eased onward. "Okay, I get it. We're not there yet. How about this? I'm pretty sure you are involved in something immense and won't give it out until you trust me. I respect that. Let me lay out what I know. Then you decide if you'll fill in the blanks afterward. Here's what I believe.

"The victims seem to have been killed by those mystery microbes. Let's call them Alphas for now, the first discovered. I'm positive that your work is about them and you have survived somehow. That about right?"

As though not expecting even a nod, she went on making her case. "Okay, so, if they are killing people to stay hidden, they must have a pretty sinister purpose. Right? They have a purpose, don't they?"

Rory took a few breaths, shocked at the question. A purpose? he asked himself. It took him and his team weeks of working with the Alphas, and they'd never questioned whether they had a purpose. "Y... Y... Yes. Well, no. It's, *uhh*, it's..." He paused, fearing he'd already gone too far. "It's complicated."

"So, if we accept that the viruses are killing the researchers, then the big issue is why. What's going on with them? I can't get enough white or black data to form a theory of any kind. But now I have to ask, and I know you won't want to answer, what are you doing at Reyton? It's all about them, isn't it?"

After a long pause, he said, "Yes," and then added, "Well, not exactly." Then there was another long silence. Rory steadied himself; revealing his secret wasn't going to be easy. It was far too immense to sum up in a few sentences. He, too, had to build a case while believing fully it would be his undoing. But of far greater weight, he would be dooming his project and workmates, too. Still, to his surprise, he trusted her, at least to a point.

Turning to the wall, he said, "Coffee black," commanding the maker. Then to his guest, "This is going to take a while." He prepped himself from habit, as though getting ready to deliver an important lecture, reviewing mentally the logical steps to his amazing conclusion.

After many deep breaths, he steeled himself to tell the convoluted tale of Reyton, its silent sponsors, the Triad, and especially about his original work there. There was no turning back. He was about to give this stranger nearly all, but not everything, and based on nothing more than a feeling. He hoped his thinking wasn't clouded by how good she'd felt against him, her soft hands upon his face, those deep-green eyes, and especially how she smelled.

Clearly, it had.

Chapter 8

Mission Collision

RORY STOOD, PULLED his bed down, and then flipped it over, forming his desk-table. He then slid the singular stool her way. "Your turn to sit." Handing her the one and only mug, he said, "Hope you don't mind sharing. You take anything in it?"

"No thanks. Just as it comes from the pot, please."

He was grateful for her answer, for he actually had nothing to put in her coffee. Black was his choice, too! At least they had that in common.

Standing above Jo-J, her dull Nandy jumpsuit now zipped partway down, he poured and couldn't avoid noticing she was young, perhaps in her late twenties. Like him, oddly enough, she, too, had red hair, but her bright-green eyes far outshone his blues. Beneath her jumpsuit, Rory half saw and half imagined what supported it so seductively. No doubt, Jo-J was female. He forgave himself for being a bit too observant: it was the first time he'd had a woman in his room since... he couldn't remember when.

Jo-J looked around and saw Rory looking at her. Their eyes locked. Rory reached desperately for the professorial control that had helped him resist all cute young co-eds back in his lectures, trying not to let this moment get to his head. But it did. Throughout the many lonely years since college graduation, there had been no companion in his life. And here was one who easily passed for a high-dollar model or escort, face to face with him, not looking away.

She could no doubt feel his hand shaking as he took the mug from her for one swallow. As he passed it back, he said, "Okay, you are right. Reyton is a bio-tech project. But before I explain what we're doing and why, you must promise me. You cannot reveal any of it ever! *Promise me.*" Silently, she nodded. "Now, put your augment on standby and never return it to the Lace."

"Oh, you needn't worry about that!" she said. "I told you I had but you were still, *uhh*, still 'warming up to me.'" She avoided referencing his fainting, which salved his ego. "I realized I had to keep it offline some time ago."

"Sorry. I should have known, when your letter told me to stay off the Lace, you'd have gone dark, too." He turned to the critical question. "What is the number one shortage in the world today?"

"*Uhh*, maybe clean water in the underdeveloped nations." But after processing her answer a bit more, she said, "Maybe not. I read in the last Mylar that the Regents are using Mason energy to force dirty water through giant reverse-osmosis dams, to clean it up." She added, "Okay, there could be several. Individual privacy maybe. How about all the unrest in South America? Geez, I don't know. You tell me."

"It has nothing to do with Mason converters, but it has everything to do with society. Bad question. Let me rephrase it. What's the number one shortage in the Uni world today?"

Her face brightened. "Well, I guess it's the fact that we haven't heard from them in a while. Did they run out of edicts and inventions?" Homing in on her answer, she said, "Hey, I just realized, we haven't had a sweeping tech upgrade in several months, right?"

"Yes, that's it exactly!" Smart girl, he thought. "Some time ago, those stupid DCS bulletins coming to all the people had nearly nothing to announce. That's because there's nothing much that's new! Little stuff, like changeable clothing, but no new processor-driven devices or programs. The worthless Mylars still come but say almost nothing!"

Sitting up, she blurted, "I see it now! Progress has stopped!"

Rory gestured. "Right you are, Joey. Can I call you that? The people haven't had to adapt to anything in months! The developed world is heading directly at a cliff, with Uni at the controls. They've created a technical freight train that's about to crash. All infrastructure and commerce today is based on change! But technical progress is based on what?

"As told to me by the Triad, technical change has become the drug that dulls the Regents' oppressive role. They invent to dull their pain. Then, because they need someone to use their new stuff, they force them upon all of us! Faster and faster, just like an addiction, they change everything. Okay, some of it is good, but most is just plain useless.

"So, the really bad part is the people have been trained to accept this. They expect change. The world has become dependent upon change, all driven by the Regents, though, not by need."

Jo-J interjected, "You know, things change so fast these days, it feels impossible sometimes. I just want my world to be the same for a while, to stop adapting. We've accepted fast rollover as normal, but I see it's not. But what has this got to do with those viruses?"

"Excellent," he said. "That's the right question! By the way, I like your idea. We'll refer to them as the Alpha virus, the first ones to exhibit behavior." Realizing he'd set the stage for the big revelation, he dove in. "If adaptation stops, and it actually has, the whole economic world will crash. I'm betting the social world will, too. Just like an addict, the population will withdraw. Soon, you'll see real craving, as the world's economy crashes, dragging society with it.

"But my Reyton planners saw all this coming early on. Reyton intends to capitalize on the problem. But that doesn't answer my question. The people behind Reyton, the Triad, have figured out a solution to get change rolling again."

"So that's what you are doing at Reyton?"

"Yes, but in a very roundabout way. Here's a critical question—why has change stopped? What's the underlying reason? And what must happen for rapid technical change to happen once again?"

"*Umm*, faster processors in devices? All this technical crud, it's all driven by central processing units in everything. They have been getting smaller, faster, and denser, right?"

"Right again. Processor chips are the epicenter of the issue. Early on, the Regents knew they had to control computer-chip evolution, if they were to control and accelerate adaptation. Originally, they bought chip makers, but then they commandeered the holdouts. Uni rounded up and controlled all processor chip making in the world. The whole crazy system is— *Uhh* no, *was* driven by smaller, denser, and faster processors. And Uni controlled it all." Rory paused for effect. "Until now. Here's a key—while it hasn't been announced and may not be, since it challenges the Regents' dominion, they've hit the *small wall*. Like all evolutionary paths, there are diminishing returns toward an eventual end."

Joey nodded, showing some understanding. "I know, in nature, everything that grows has a determinant height— everything! So I see Uni is no different, although their limit isn't overgrowth. It is smallness. Using their family of decreasingly smaller bots to make chips, they simply can't get smaller. They've come to the end! There cannot be smaller omega-bots or denser processors. But can't we make molecular devises? I know that's possible. And what about quantum computers…?"

"Oh, that's already been done, too. Nine months ago, the final SFD processor was created and introduced. The small wall ended at the molecular level.

"But my Reyton planners saw it early on. Reyton intends to capitalize on the problem. You see, they were among the resentful companies ripped away by the Regents."

"Okay, so, what is Reyton doing? You can't be serious. They— I mean *your* team is planning to use viruses in place of bots to make computer chips, aren't they?"

"You got it. But, try as we may, we couldn't get the Alphas to bend to our will. The answer was to use what we knew and create another brilliant virus. We arrogantly thought we could use their DNA and create a new virus that would work for us. Here's how they thought we would pull it off."

"There's more?"

"If we succeeded in training our virus to do our work, then a new phase would begin—producing nanoparticle processor chips. Then, being the only supplier, the Triad intended to blackmail Uni as the only way to get their technical world changing again. But that wasn't enough. They wanted payback. Their ultimate goal was, shortly thereafter, they would amass enough credats, control, and clout to overthrow Uni! Overthrow Uni," he repeated. "And the hell of all this is they wanted me to force the virus to do it."

"Did you?"

We started to, but as we progressed, something changed drastically. We began by creating an environment in which the Alphas could exist without host cells. Then, isolating them in our comfy fluid environment, we began to do two things. We investigated that unusual appendage to find it was a real brain. We realized that intelligence has no lower limit and the Alphas were intelligent. Not smart like a dog or dolphin. I mean self-aware—smart like you and me. Or more!

"Next, we began communication. Slowly, we actually became closer to them. But as we did so, we ended up with a whole new perspective on our work and a whole new virus!"

"New virus? Hasn't that been done already? I know the genome was solved thirty years ago. We've mapped and cataloged every chromosome, right? When I was just a little girl." This stung Rory just a little. "Science predicted they would be able to make living tissue from ingredients."

"Not yet," he told her. "Everything that's been done since mapping, all the sequences, all the data gathered in all these years has been to take some living entity, or a piece of one, and modify it. We've spliced and inserted and removed genes. We've repaired broken sequences, swapped them, and made modified entities. Even made RNA into DNA. But in every single instance, every single revision had parents. We've always started with life to morph it into another form. Not once, not ever have we created life from scratch—not even once!" Rory said with emphasis.

"Until now, no matter how many times biologists tried, myself included, we couldn't start with raw materials, add organic ooze and electricity, and then conjure up anything living. We've come close, where materials organize into cellular structures, but there was always that vital missing spark! Nothing divided into a copy of itself.

"We weren't after animal tissue much less something sentient. In all those years, all we'd been trying to do was create from ingredients cells that reproduce, progeny without progenitors."

Rory paused then started down another path. "You probably know from your math studies that, in all sciences, there are fundamental properties we keep running into. They are answers to questions we cannot derive—not unlike your blackest data. In physics, astrophysics, mathematics, and all other sciences, there always seems to be one basic question at the bottom of all questions, where we've bored down to one big blockade. But the heck of it is, it underlies all we know.

"By blocks I mean it's beyond our human ability to answer or, perhaps more to the point, for us to understand. So, after admitting we just ran up against the final property, we invent a theory we can live with, then go back up the question chain until we're back at a comfortable level where the answers make sense. We scientists make it into something that sounds scientific. We call it a theory, but really it's PFM—Pure Fucking Magic!

"For example, in your field, mathematics, what happened when someone asked about the square root of a negative number?"

"We use 'I', an imaginary digit."

"Yes, but that's because no mathematical genius could find an answer within the framework of understanding, so they invented the imaginary number and symbolized it as 'I' slipped in a solution whenever they need it. But PFM might be a more honest symbol!"

Joey could wait no longer, for she, too, had a bombshell of an announcement. First, she summed up what Rory had told her. "Okay, so, your work was to train these Alpha viruses to make chips. And when you did, the Triad would take over the world. Did you ever consider what would happen to you and your team if you succeeded?"

Rory gave her no answer, but his eyes widened.

"I want to hear all the rest, but I, too, have something to tell you that will rock your world. What I have to say will be a total challenge to what you've told me this far!"

Curious, Rory finished quickly. "Arrogantly, try as we might, we just couldn't create life. It never happened. To our amazement, it seemed very much like we were blocked by some secret code. It seemed the formula was proprietary, almost as though..." He let his sentence hang, not wanting to say the words Intelligent Design, Creator, or the final one, God.

"We had to finally accept, if one takes a pile of blueprints for, let's say, an airplane, and then lays them down, would they build the plane? Of course not. And neither could the data in the DNA build a sentient being. Microbiologists postulated that something above DNA was directing the work. We named it the *'epigenome,'* a force working above the genome." He wisely withheld the word "entity" above the genome. "We just weren't privy to the intelligence required to do anything as brilliant as the epigenome.

"Looking further, we discovered chemical strands associated with the core of the chromosomes—up the middle. We noticed, when DNA divides in cells, the chemical markers in the strands change. We thought we had it. Those strands were directing the work.

"But again we hit a wall. It came to pass that the strands were simply the result of the higher Epi, doing its work. A sort of progress chart or record. Something had to be using the DNA data and making cells become all the differing tissues in any living thing. It's a super-high function.

"It's common knowledge there's almost no difference in one's chromosomes, one person to the next, yet we're wildly diverse. Something directs that... what? In fact, there's less than two percent genetic difference between us and apes. It's pretty skilled work. The epigenome plays a key role in all living things, and it remained a mystery fundamental."

Joey gasped. "You figured it out, broke through, didn't you? You made life! How?"

"Not exactly." Rory sucked in a last breath before disclosing his monumental secret. With no turning back he plunged, into the fantastic event. "Lucy, Artie, and I didn't actually make new life, but we set up the conditions and especially the will, such that new life sprang forth. We have been witness to the making of new life—very, very special new life. We fostered it!" he said with deep pride.

"Once we began to communicate with them, we came to see we couldn't let the original goal happen. They may be small, but they're real beings. Not bugs, but genuine entities that deserve to live.

"We began with simple signals into the tank, using math as a basis, at first. Then, employing ascending symbols and eventually words, we began real conversations with what were proving to be our equals! Our equals," he repeated. With that, he stopped talking. The message was just too much for someone even as plucky and bright as Joey to absorb in one gulp.

"Now you. It's your turn to amaze me. I doubt you can top that. But I also can't go further without my team present. It's their project, too."

Chapter 9

Startling Truth

JOEY STOOD. "Okay," she said, "but it's your turn to sit. I'm pretty sure what I'm about to tell you is far more startling than what you've just told me! I'm not kidding—sit down!" She motioned then waited.

Taking one deep breath to compose herself, she plunged into just what she'd promised: a fantastic set of facts of which she was ninety-percent sure. "While I don't have the science behind me, as you do, I believe I've uncovered more than just your whereabouts and the possibility you and I may be next to be slain. I don't think it's the Triad. It's the Alphas trying to remain covert. I'm almost positive, given all the dead scientists. Think about it. They, too, had Alphas in them, didn't they?"

"Of course, but how—?"

Knowing the next question, she interrupted. "But that's not even close to the hellishness of what I have to convince you of." She pushed on. "I'm ninety-percent sure that the Alphas intend to end the human race!"

Rory half rose, spilling the last of the coffee., "Oh, come on. That's just crazy. Genocide? All thirteen billion?" He blurted out, "Why in the hell would they do that? They live in us. If we die, so do they!"

"Let me explain. Mine takes a bit of foundation-laying, too. In trying to make sense of all the evidence I' uncovered, I wondered what was killing the scientists. Then I realized that some entity had something to hide. Slowly, I had to admit it was actually the virus they were studying. I'm pretty sure they have an escape plan for the time when they kill us all, and I'm also sure you won't like it.

"Baffled about their purpose, I sought answers in human history. Here's what I uncovered. In the beginning, the Earth was uninhabitable. Then, magically, your Alphas appeared and, I suspect, shortly thereafter other micro-entities that the Alphas created. " She repeated, "That they created!

"Then came cellular life, enough to get the biosphere humming. Animate life evolved larger and larger until the dinosaurs. Now, this is a leap, but I see them, along with the paleo-plant life sustaining them, as the forward scouts, the big machines prepping the Earth for a long succession of life phases. The dinos were suddenly wiped out. Science says it was from an impact, but was it? I think not. I believe it was the Alphas behind the entire evolution!"

Again, she let this theory sink in. After a moment, she continued. "They just didn't need the dinosaurs any longer and did away with them! Other species followed, all toward their goal. With our stupidity, we are wiping out species, too, but we're no longer needed in their plan, so we're doing the dirty work for them.

"Next came myriad experiments with large, warm-blooded animals that had varying degrees of intelligence. Mammoths, for example. Then, with each revision, animals and plants, too, became smaller. Animals became pretty smart, leading to mankind. You can graph it—most living creatures became smaller and smarter. Mankind is at the end of the chain thus far. Self-determinate. We can deduce, invent, and we are creative. And I'm pretty sure I know why they created us that way—yes, I did say 'created.' I believe the Alphas are our creators!"

Rory tried to process Joey's unbelievable tale while also trying to reject it. Her theory contradicted everything he believed to be true.

She went on. "But here's the bad part, as if it isn't enough to discover we've been made by super-intelligent microbes. Rory, I believe we're not the last revision. There's one more. When that happens, we'll go the way of the dinosaurs, no longer needed."

"Okay, wait just a minute," Rory interjected. "Why would they do that?"

"You think I'm crazy, don't you? Just listen." She was flushed and excited to finally be able to tell someone. Although completely uncharacteristic for this strong woman, she reverted to girlish behavior just once and coyly asked, "Would you mind terribly if I take off this ugly jumpsuit?"

"Sure, no problem!" Rory replied, thinking she was clothed beneath it.

Joey unzipped fully and wriggled until the suit fell, revealing a freckled body swathed only in small panties.

Rory struggled, his old professor skills falling to the floor along with her jumpsuit. He stammered, "Wow! Oh God, I'm so sorry I said that. It's just that—"

She held up both palms. "Don't. I understand. You've been alone a long time. Me, too. But, if I'm right and we work out how our two truths coincide, then we'll be together in some pretty rough life-and-death situations. We'll see lots of each other intimately, so let's get beyond that, okay?"

Nodding, Rory gave her what she needed to know, but inwardly he wasn't so sure. Joey was stunning in every way!

"Okay, let's start combining your revelations with mine," she suggested. "Along with human evolution getting technically smarter, aren't computer chips doing the same? Smarter and smaller? Isn't that a coincidence?" she asked rhetorically.

"Sure." Rory was trying to see the big picture. "I see it. They are?"

"So now, don't you see, if your Triad is successful in making the absolute smallest electronic devises, couldn't the little guys that made them then use them? If I'm right, if the Reyton project succeeds at making the smallest chips conceivable, then we would be obsolete—the human race no longer needed! But if I'm hearing you right, they haven't made them yet, the chips—right?"

"Nobody made them, but not because we couldn't train the Alphas. We stalled simply because it dawned on us, had we finished our task, an organization of power-hungry men with no good intentions would gain world control. So we did busy work, which wasn't exactly what we were supposed to do, but the results are perhaps the most amazing secret yet."

Pausing a bit, Rory almost shouted, "Crap! Both stories, yours and mine, lead to a bad conclusion. Mine ends with society as slaves to the Triad and probable death for me and my team, and yours leads to total analyzation of us all, and, worse, it gives me no hope of changing it!"

Joey asked, "How can we possibly face down our creator? The Triad, the Uni—both are fragile humans. With luck and scheming, we can overcome them, but the very entity that gave us life is far smarter than us, living within us, and well below our ability to confront. Can't be done!"

She had come to Rory out of hope, so she added, "I don't know the whole answer but, working with your team, we might, if we keep seeing how the two sets of facts dovetail. Maybe?" She gestured with both palms out, letting her idea hang. Rory tried to not look between her hands.

Joey noticed his discomfort at her exposed body and liked it, for she had been alone for some time, too. "The next revision, Mankind 2.0, would need to be more subservient, less self-directed. A pack animal, much smaller, but this time not nearly as intelligent, or at least not like we are.

"In my opinion," she continued, "the Alphas totally screwed up in creating us. They hadn't counted on two things. First, thinking they made us far less intelligent than we are, I believe they didn't envision any human uncovering their self-serving plot. Secondly, the humans they made needed to be self-guiding and inventive if they— *we* were to create the smallest chips ever. But again, they missed the fact that we'd turn to viruses to make what they needed! What a convoluted situation. They created us, and we're using them... Or at least Reyton thought that's what they would do.

"Rory, not only do you need to keep Reyton from succeeding to prevent the Triad taking control of the world, you absolutely must stop particle chips to save the human race! So, have I convinced you?"

Chapter 10

Focus on Survival

RORY FELL SILENT. Minutes, maybe hours passed. Joey paced, waiting for any kind of response, as he lowered his head to the table.

"Give me a minute. I gotta think."

"Fine. But do you have anything to eat?"

"Look in the unit. I have enough for one day. It seems to show up every day, though I don't know how."

As time passed, she heard him almost snoring. She tapped his head. With no small effort, he lifted it.

Still chewing the Unidentified Food Object found in his unit, she said, "First off, your team just got bigger. I'm here to stay. Do we have the whole solution or even a partial one? I know I don't, and I need you to think through what I've told you and combine it with your truths. I have them all, don't I?"

Studying Rory's sleepy eyes, she could see he hadn't completely finished. She went on. "So, in the short term, we must do what you're doing now, dragging your feet, not letting the chips get made. The Alphas don't get their chips from Reyton. But given they've been on this quest for millennia, do you think the little bastards will just give up if Reyton doesn't supply them?

"In fact, do you think you are the only Reyton-like project? Surely they'll keep on trying until someone falls into their trap! They've shown themselves to be patient beyond imagination. If

I'm right, and I'm pretty sure I am, this plot started millennia ago. We won't solve it today or tomorrow, but we will fight back!"

Noting he was going in and out of focus, she added, "Look, it's late. You've been without sleep for days, and I've been sleeping among the homeless, dodging the Uni. I'm exhausted, too. Let's sleep on it, eh? We can start early tomorrow. I need time to think, and I can see you aren't thinking at all. Okay?"

Trying to sound cavalier, Rory said, "Okay, fine. I'm exhausted and probably not capable of good thought. But, missy, I have only one bed and no couch!"

As a liberated woman, she had no issue with one bed. In fact, that was her goal, but she recoiled at the term "missy," for it meant he saw her not as an equal.

Rory grasped for his student-avoidance skills that had protected him when willing co-eds signed up for his lectures. But they were failing him.

A proven decisive woman, Joey decided on the spot to change their relationship for good. She sternly announced, "Look, Rory, if we might die trying to save mankind, don't you think we ought to share ourselves with each other? We need to be genuinely entwined. You understand—equal partners. Equal!"

He tried but words just wouldn't come, so he just nodded what might have been a hundred-degree *yes*. He flipped the table and pulled back the covers as she quietly walked behind him to unbutton then drop his Uni-form. For the second time, she pressed her breasts against him, smooth soft. Jo-J took charge of their first night together.

Trembling, he turned to face her parted lips and green eyes. "I, *uhh*, I— I haven't been with a woman for a, *uhh*, well, for a very long time. You are so beautiful and, and... Well you, you..." He grasped at words. "I wouldn't think someone so beautiful would—"

Her palms up again, she stopped him then lunged!

Trying to say he wasn't sure he was worthy or maybe that he wouldn't be able to satisfy her youthful needs, Rory was dazed at the fast unfolding. It had been so long, and she was so sweet but strong at the same time—so much more than he could have dreamed would ever be attracted to him.

But in that wonderful moment, he knew—it wasn't going to be a problem! Not even!

Chapter 11

Escape Planning

AFTER HIS YEARS of abstinence and her weeks of loneliness, both Rory and Joey desperately anticipated warm skin on skin. But total exhaustion trumped all that, and they both fell asleep instantly. Unconsecrated, they slept in each other's arms until thin dawn.

Using its morning voice, Rory's cubicle server cheerfully announced, *"Doctor Enetie, it's two thirty. Time to get up."*

Opening his eyes, Rory saw his reflection in Joey's sleepy deep greens, framed in her flowing red hair. She was above him, awake. With anticipation and after a good night's sleep, Jo-J slid on top of him with moves no college girl had ever come close to having. Hungrily, she lowered her open mouth on his.

Rory for the first time was going to be late getting to the Reyton lab. He would need to explain, but not now. "You do see that the shower is just a curtain in the corner."

"This room isn't made for two." She smiled. "Got soap?" Reluctantly, she rolled over him, stood, and then pulled him up to her. "It might be a little tight, but I bet we can shower together!"

Flushed, they wheeled around and dove back in the tiny bed.

Blissful minutes passed. "I'm feeling so guilty!" he said, exhaling.

"Why?"

"We have the fate of the human race on us, and here we are, balling like animals in heat!"

"So what?" Then she added, "The world won't end today. And don't we both deserve a little time to ourselves and some happiness? Besides, Mister Rory, I'm not balling, and neither are you. We're making love, and if anything sets us apart from the animals, and probably the Alphas, too, it's love. I don't think we can win this battle, saving mankind, if we aren't doing it with and for love."

Staring at his knees, Rory sheepishly agreed. "I... I'm not very good at relationships. Actually, I'm terrible at them. Never really had one. Forgive me?"

"Of course. And more, I'm about to say something one is never to say on the first date, especially on the first morning after sleeping with someone." She giggled. "Even if it was really just sleep." She sat up straight and stood above where he lay across the bed. "Doctor Enetie... Or should I call you Tinette? I know myself pretty well and have never said this to anyone before. Rory, I love you! I know I do. Is that crazy? After one night?"

"Not as crazy as this," he replied. "I think I love you, too! I've never felt this way, not once." Then, although it seemed a little anticlimactic, he added, "Just call me Rory!"

A small tear slid down her cheek as she began to say, "Last night, as I was falling asleep— sorry about that." He let that slide, because he was asleep before her. "I had a big question. If everyone has Alphas in them, don't you and your lab assistants, too?"

"Yes, we do. But, because the people financing Reyton had the augments suppressed, the world knows nothing about our work. There's more to be learned when we get to the lab."

"So, your research seems to be far beyond the death-sentence tipping point. Why haven't they killed you?"

"That's a great question, and the answer is I still haven't told you everything."

She was stunned, thinking she had entered Rory's inner circle. After all, he had entered hers. "Why not?" she demanded.

"When we get to the lab and you meet Lucy, she'll explain the rest. I direct the research, but she did the daily work. Since the discovery really is to her credit, I'm not free to tell you without her. I guess I don't really need her permission, but I feel like she must be the one to tell you."

"What?"

"Can't say, and I can't believe I'm saying this, but get your jumpsuit on. I want her to tell you. I'm sure you two will really hit it off! Here, I'll help you pull it up." After another few minutes passed, the garment finally rose up over her luscious hips and was zipped closed.

Finally clothed, the new lovers walked out to the platform and headed for Reyton, each with a whole new understanding of what the lab held in store for mankind.

"I can hardly wait to introduce you to Lucy and Artie!" Rory said with excitement. "They'll already be there now, no doubt wondering what's happened to me. If Reyton was a normal workshop, we'd just Lace our situation to them. But we stay totally in the shadows, by careful design."

"Don't need to tell me," she said. "Remember all it took to find you. I had to invent a whole new analysis tool just to do it!" Waiting for the tube car to arrive, she smiled up at Rory. "We fit together pretty good, don't you think? And I'm betting we'll work together even better. Don't you?"

He crafted his answer, for he knew it meant a lot to Joey. "Absolutely. Under normal circumstances, an affair would make teamwork difficult. But, given the impossibility of what we've got to do, in this case I agree. If it's not for love, then what's the use? Well, shit, I did it again, didn't I? It's *not* an affair! Listen, you'll need to be patient with me in the romance department." A broad smile crossed his face. "I guess you're my love professor." Satisfied with his answer, he added, "Together, we might be able to figure out what to do. So, while we ride to Reyton, prep yourself to condense the two stories into one and make it believable."

Swooshing air announced that the vacuum tube train had arrived. The door slid open, and, trying to not look like lovers, they entered. They eyed each other then quickly looked away. The short ride was torturous for both.

Arriving one stop short of the Nandy platform, Rory directed Joey to follow him, adding by way of explanation, "We never get off at our stop."

They stepped into the fog. Rory waited until they were away, walking the half mile toward 15-19, to ask, "Joey, I have a small question. How in the world did you get that envelop into the DCS conveyor and delivered to me at Reyton?"

In a low voice, she replied, "It was so simple. It was pretty evident nobody gives a damn about the DCS. There are no guards at the terminal, no surveillance. Not even a locked door! The place is freaky—mostly automated, with only a few jump-suited low-levels, and I had mine on. No kidding, I just walked around with a broom until I found the pallet stack for Nandy then slipped it into the right sort for 15-19. About the only way anyone was going to detect me would have been if one of the AI vans scanned me, but they were out on day shift." She gestured. "In and out. It was surprisingly easy!"

Nearing their lab, Rory directed Joey to walk opposite him in the alley, and then to cross just as he stopped. Despite thinking the secrecy measures a bit overdone, she obeyed. When she met back up with him in front of N15-19, he commanded the door open.

The office server had a new delight, a visitor! Its very first since being booted.

Observing her hooded figure in the lobby, the server slid the door closed, keeping the mist outside. Cheerfully, it greeted her. "Welcome to Reyton Manufacturing," it said, sounding almost proud.

Rory was still getting used to "her" voice. He knew it was sexist to refer to the assistant with a gender, but, being institutionalized by age, he couldn't help himself. No pet names yet for her, though. And since Reyton was now on a fast track to doom, he probably never would name her.

"Lights low, windows opaque," he commanded. Taking Joey by the hand, he lead her through the innocent first portal and headed to the gauntlet. For the first time, he truly enjoyed the whole process. Together, they stripped, endured the sequential chambers, and finally came to the showers.

Sensing a female, the internal program adapted to Lucy's physiology and began to probe and scrub in places as Rory tried to not watch. Feeling embarrassed and maybe a bit lecherous but oddly heated at the near-pornographic scene, he actually did watch before, red-faced, he turned away from Joey and identified himself to the reader. The air lock cycled, and they walked into the inner chamber.

Alarms chimed and red light flashed, startling Lucy and Artie, who were already getting ready for the day's discussion with their new friends.

Lucy sprang forward. "Rory, who the hell is that?"

Gesturing to both of them, he pleaded, "Please. Come over here and sit down. I have a lot to tell you. And please try to understand, I just learned it myself. It's something we never suspected, and it's so very important! But first, meet Joey Jaydon. She's our new partner. Her associates back at the University of Washington call her Jo-J. She has information that's going to change everything we believed we were doing."

Waiting a bit, he continued, "We've been horribly used by the Triad, but when you hear her complete story, you'll see we've been used even worse by, *uhm*, by... Well, by... by others." He just couldn't say "by the virus" just yet.

"But let me have her tell it. And yes, I know I've violated my own rules. Nobody finds out about Reyton. But the point is she already had and has the real truth! She found me."

"Everything?" Artie stammered. "The *entire* truth?"

"Not all of it, but neither did we, until she arrived. I'm not sure that even by combining hers and ours we'll have it all. I can just say you two have a lot to learn! When you do have the whole picture, you'll see we've got a huge task ahead of us! Much bigger than making nano-chips. But we must all be on the same page. So much depends on it. Her half and ours combined—everything will depend on our taking action!" he stressed.

Rory desperately wanted to finish the sentence with, "saving the human race," but he knew he and Jo-J had to build the fantastic story in stages, just as she had done for him. Had she told him any other way, he, too, would have flat-out rejected it. But he also knew that the biggest shocker was still ahead for her.

Rory carefully watched his assistants for their reaction, suspecting resistance. "Okay, Joey," he said. "Go ahead."

Artie noticed their familiarity but seemed open-minded about Rory's relationship with this newcomer. Lucy, however, folded her arms in a gesture clearly announcing to the "competition" that she was ready to do battle. True to his gender, Rory totally missed that, not having any idea Lucy had feelings for him, too.

In stages, Jo-J wove the tale told to Rory: about the scientists dying as soon as they began to learn about the special viruses' behavior. She explained data reversal and how it had worked to find them.

Then she said, "I'm ninety percent sure that the tipping point came as each scientist asked themselves what their purpose is. I'm one-hundred percent sure, they do have goals, and if I'm right, you won't like them! But more, the human race won't like them. They, not the Triad, want— no, they *need* the nano-chips." Then she dropped the nuke. "They planned all along from the very beginning of life on Earth to create a miniature world that they could manage.

"They are geniuses at bio-engineering but have no clue about electro-mechanical devices. They made us, we humans, able to do those things for them." Pausing, since the next revelation would be the big one, she then said, "As much as you and I don't want to believe it, I'm sure we're their assistants. Slaves might be a better term!"

She added, "In the entire series of animate life and the plants that sustained them, which evolved through each epoch, the entire eco-system was designed and created by these viruses, always with a goal of miniaturizing communication to the point where they could use it.

"As life slowly evolved toward their goal, their latest revision of the human race needed to be more intelligent and self-directed, possessing the smarts and drive to finally create their microscopic chips. We were supposed to finish their long-awaited result.

"But they made a big mistake in designing mankind. We're too self-determining. We have the will to live and the intelligence to adapt. They created us in their own image, just a bit too much. We became too intelligent. It's all so convoluted. All life including mankind was struggling upward, working toward their plan."

Rory could remain silent no longer. "So you see, when we began trying to train viruses to make the chips, we were actually obeying their master plan. But it totally looped back upon them when we turned to viruses to do it!"

"Lucy," Joey said, "Rory tells me you're the communication expert. Why didn't they just tell you it was them, not the Triad, that wanted you to make small chips?"

Lucy had an odd smirk on her face but didn't answer. Boy, have we got something to tell you." She gestured to Joey. "Go ahead. Finish your thought."

"Oh wait, I think I can answer my own question. As they always did, they hid the role reversal. But I have another question. How did you learn to communicate with them in the first place?"

Rory pointed. "Artie, you're the systems expert. Tell her how we got started."

"Okay," he explained. "After the viruses became comfortable with their new surroundings, we began with modulated light. We sent good old Morse Code flashes. They could flash back in color waves produced by millions of them working together. That totally blew our mind, and we knew we were on to something really big. First ever contact!

"It worked okay for basic numbers and symbols." It was his turn to be proud of their progress, as he pushed on. "We followed the first-contact protocol, starting with math as the key. Then we elevated to words both we and they could relate to, like death, food, and child. Finally, with a growing vocabulary, we strung words together into thoughts. Clumsy, to say the least, but we were actually communicating!" He nodded at Lucy. "You're the one doing the actual communication now. Tell her the rest."

Lucy glared at Joey. "Okay, as we progressed, we all felt that the fast learning curve wasn't so much because of us as it was them leading the way. Eventually, we discussed how we could improve communication. They told us they were aware of the neural connections to our augments. We told them we'd had them disconnected by the Triad. And that started a whole series of similar events, starting with saying they had a better idea. I can't overstress how smart they are. So, they told me they could go back within each of us and re-code our defunct augments. We could scrap the clumsy light flashes.

"But then it became even more freaky when they told me, before they did, there was something they had to do. We had no clue as to what it was until you came to fill in the blanks. But now I know. We already knew they liked us, but with your new perspective, I see clearly they had come to realize that the Alpha plan was just wrong. They had concluded, through our new connection, they no longer wanted to enslave us but wanted to be our friends. I now believe that they disavowed the Alpha plan!"

Rory spoke up. "But then, if you think about it, ours was a pretty awful plan, too! We were going to enslave them, or at least the Triad thought we could. We've come to see that not even if we were given a million more years would we be able to do that."

Artie added, "I think that's my favorite part of working with them. We keep learning. Our new friends can always come up with a better way. They are so inventive. But to re-enter our cells wasn't easy. In fact, it was downright awful for both parties."

Joey was puzzled by this. "Well, if they are so darned smart, why didn't they just make the chips themselves?"

"Hmm, let me think about that...," Rory said. "Crew, have you got the answer?"

Artie offered, "Well, keep in mind we'd only made the final molecular omega bot chips at this point. They probably looked bigger than skyscrapers to them—down at their resolution. So, it was getting closer to their scale but still far too big."

Rory stood. "Right, Artie. Thanks. Okay, both of you. It's time to see where we stand together. I know it's too much to ask and may lead to our death, but Joey and I believe we must try to stop them from getting their chips. But, if you want to walk out now, I promise I won't stop you. And I promise, as much as it's up to me, you'll be safe from the Triad. But no guarantees. As far as safe from the Alphas, that's anyone's guess."

Breathing hard, he waited, watched, and hoped.

Turning to Rory, in unison both Lucy and Artie demanded, "You really *believe* her?"

"Yes, I do. Completely. *Everything!*" he emphasized. "I've always had a weird feeling something was missing, some fact just out of our reach, and I believe she's discovered it. We've been working for evil viruses that could care less about mankind.

"We need to be a team to fight back, and I believe we can, if we enlist our new friends. But it'll be beyond dangerous. If you agree to stay, then we need to fill her in about them. I haven't told her the final truth yet. I needed to get this far before I did. So I ask you—are you with us or not?"

"New friends?" Joey asked.

"Yes, there's more, but it's so secret I wasn't willing to reveal it outside the lab, even to you. See, I'm not positive I'm not monitored in my cubicle. And I needed my team's permission to tell you anyway."

Lucy's angst boiled within as she heard Rory admit that her competition had been inside his place the night before, something she would have gladly done but never gotten the invitation.

He repeated, "I've got to know are you in or out? And I promise, as much as I can control, if you decide to go, I'll do what I can to protect you."

Artie, a risk-taker by nature, accepted his boss's word completely. But, clouded by jealousy, Lucy remained undecided.

Scowling toward Joey, her claws fully out, she said as a challenge, "Miss Jaydon... Or should I call you Jo-J? Or Joey?" Nodding at clueless Rory, Lucy continued, "What exactly have you two decided to do with this truth? Exactly! What will we be doing about it? And exactly what's between you two?"

Finally, Rory caught on. "Yes, Lucy, we're more than teammates." Placing his arm around Joey's shoulder, he added, "A lot more!" The rest was left unsaid, but he hoped that falling for Jo-J hadn't destroyed his team. "Please don't doubt her motives."

Then Rory tried to move beyond the awkward moment. "Lucy, I'm not sure what we can do, if anything. And if there's any hope, it's up to them to help us. But Luce, I just can't without your okay." He turned to face to Lucy. "For the last time, in or out?"

"Rory, that's not fair. Two hours ago, everything was crystal clear. Since we've opened real communication with the— the, *uhh*, 'new' Alphas, we thought we had a well-defined mission. Teach them to make chips and then turn it over to the Triad. We'd retire wealthy."

"Okay," Rory said, "first off, you only *think* you'd retire. I'm almost certain the Triad planned to kill us once we completed the Alpha training and they got their chips. But now you see the viruses were planning to kill us, too! We three and now Joey are in a shit sandwich. Not a hopeful scenario, huh?"

Lucy continued to press him. "So now you tell me they created us? Not for love or good but to do their bidding? We're their minions?"

"That's right, Luce. And if you can accept that horrible truth, can you see yourself staying with us to fight back? You're the prime communicator on our team. We'll need you to work with our new friends, if we're to have any hope of surviving. It's a genuine crusade to save the human race!" Rory pleaded.

"Another piece of bad news," he added, "as if all this isn't, is while we won't be supplying the trained chip-making crew to the Triad, or for the Alphas either, after listening to Joey, I'm convinced that some entity will. The viruses have stuck to this plan for millions of years, here on Earth. Talk about patience. They won't give up just because we refused to help them. I'm certain the next try won't be the Triad. As rich as they are, they won't be able to finance another Reyton.

"But, given the change withdrawal that the Uni is undergoing, I'm sure they'll set up a lab of their own. Who knows? One way or another, somebody is going to invent a supply of nano-chips. And whoever they are, they probably won't see they are actually working for the Alphas! We would have never seen it, if it wasn't for Joey and her coincidental research. They will get their communication tools! But the question is what will *we* do about this?"

Motivated by Rory's speech, Artie stood. "Okay—yes. I'm in!" he pledged. "Holy cow, here I go, rebelling against the three most powerful enemies on Earth— a Triad of three super-power-hungry men, a Uni of five blindsided geeks, and billions upon billions of evil viruses! No problem. It's a cake walk!" He swiveled around to face his lab partner. "Lucy, you up for suicide?"

"Damn It!" was all she said, and with that they became an army of four, pitted against very different, very dangerous opponents, each with its own agenda and none that held any hope for the rebelling Reyton team.

"Okay, now what?" Lucy asked weakly but trying to sound resolved. "How?"

Unable to hold back no longer, Jo-J had to ask, "You keep talking about new friends and enlisting them... Who? And, by the way, you can call me Joey. My closest friends do."

Refreshed from a night's sleep and his newly discovered love, Rory stood and paced as he spoke. "We've accomplished the most amazing breakthrough in all human history. I'm not sure you could say we created anything, but, with our help, we've made it possible for something wonderful to happen. In truth, we three have made contact with an alien race, but not on a faraway planet, as we always thought we would. We found them, *uhh...* I guess, more to the point, we helped give birth to them right here at Reyton!"

Nearly beyond speech and just a bit angry for having had to wait this long for Rory to finally bring her fully into the secrecy of Reyton, Jo-J turned to him in disbelief. "What are you—? You created viruses?"

"Joey, you've got to believe me, this is the last secret we have between us. Yes... Well, no, we didn't *create* them. That's still beyond our ability. Only the viruses themselves have the epigenome. But we did discover and foster something absolutely amazing. Lucy...?"

"Okay, it began with our growing affection for them. The *truth*," she emphasized, "between us. You recall our conversation about mankind not being able to make new life? It's true. But *they* could, the Alphas could. They did, in fact—*all* life. Organizing cellular creation, building life, using cellular division—that's their given purpose. The microchips are just a convenience they wanted. Okay, maybe they *needed* would be a better word."

"So, you are telling me the Alphas are the epigenome?" Joey asked.

Lucy replied, "Not exactly, but they have the epigenome embedded in their brains. It's really part of their super-intelligence, and so they direct the work. They trigger cells to become various tissues."

Rory beamed at Joey's comprehension while Artie's jaw dropped. It had taken them months to finally conclude the Alphas were in charge of the epigenome work in living tissue, yet Joey had seen it based merely on the sketchy evidence presented thus far!

He said, "Right you are, and Joey, when viewed from a certain perspective, the Alpha viruses were in fact mankind's guiding deity! It's a huge discovery Our Creator, our Gods are not in heaven but within us all!" Then he continued, "Okay, now we can work together. And I know where to begin. The Bios."

"Bios?" Joey asked.

Lucy turned and faced them as she chimed in. "Yes. We're calling our new friends Bios. Why not? We've named the enemy Alphas, the first, so maybe Betas would be more appropriate, but Bios sounds friendly. And aren't they our friends?"

Joey, completely mystified, stepped forward as she demanded, "What the Sam Hill are you saying?"

"Yes, that's what I said. Our friends and more," Rory replied. "This is the final shocker I promise. First, we created the tank environment in which viruses could survive outside of host cells. You probably know they can't stay alive for very long by themselves on surfaces or in the air. We solved that issue first, with our globulin fluid. It has the same properties as within a cell. Then we enticed just a few Alphas from our own bodies, to migrate into the fluid."

Joey turned to face Lucy then pointed at the big tank. "You mean Bios are in there now?" She jumped up and sprang over to it, putting her face close to the glass, where clear red fluid circulated slowly within. "I can't see them, but they are in there, aren't they?"

Lucy noticed Jo-J's very well-rounded bottom as she bent to peer into the glass. With a stinging tone, she answered, "Yes, Joey. They have willingly become Bios."

Rory took over. "Yes indeed, Joey," he stressed. "And as I was about to say, they have been reborn." Realizing he had to end the enmity between the two females, although he wanted to do the bragging, he asked Lucy to take point and unravel their amazing accomplishment. "Luce, fill her in, will you? Don't leave anything out. Artie, if you have anything to add, please feel free."

Lucy walked over to the tank. "At first, as Artie said, our conversation was pretty elementary. But it rose in depth exponentially. We began real exchanges. In fact, we can do so today. They are waiting for us."

"Oh my gosh! I get to talk to the Bios?" Joey asked, excited.

"If you are really going to be a team member, then you've got to be able to communicate with them, too. And yes, something did happen. We're almost there." Lucy pushed on. "As we got closer to them, we realized they liked their new home, the freedom from their cell life, and especially the interspecies communication. Think about their world before Reyton, each trapped in a body, not having, *uhh*, well... We like to think about it as not having any 'fun'! We literally freed them from being forever secreted away, entrapped in unfriendly giant entities.

"With little challenge in their lives, after their cellular work was finished, building whatever was on the menu—ape, boy, girl, whatever—other than some injury repair, they had little or no epigenome responsibility. They created, lived, and then died in their hosts. They raised families, and I have to believe loved their children. You'll see why in just a minute. We not only set them free, we gave them a way to communicate that had nothing to do with electronics. Well shoot, I'm ahead of myself. It's all so exciting!"

Again demonstrating her amazing insight, Joey exclaimed, "Hey, combining both stories, I see a reason for something that has bothered me my whole life—disease and aging. Those were the Alphas' control rods, part of their plan, weren't they? It was a provision to keep life under their control, especially human. They couldn't let us age forever, getting smarter and smarter. By limiting our lifespan, they assured we wouldn't outgrow our supportive role! It's a lot like the story of the tower of Babel, where God scrambled languages to keep people suppressed."

Rory nodded, even more sure this woman was the one! She was so intuitive and quick! How could he be so fortunate, undeserving, and just plain lucky?

Turning to Lucy, he said, "You see why I've invited her to join us?"

Lucy continued. "Soon, we posed the question 'What do you want?' With no idea about the Alpha goals, we asked what could we do for them? Keep in mind, until you showed up, Joey, we thought we were in the dark about their former agenda. Now I see we probably needed to ask just who is training who?

"Anyway, they said they wanted to be allowed to live in the tank and could we make more tanks for their offspring. We told them we would be happy to do that, fully believing it was a breakthrough toward the chips."

Artie laughed. "Shit, we were so ignorant, we thought we were going to train *them!*"

Lucy took the conversation back. "Artie is right, the fast-changing relationship totally amazed us. As we got closer and closer to them, we had the oddest feeling we were bonding. It was unsettling, because we weren't sure just who was the parent and who the child in the relationship, but it felt like real family. We liked them!"

As Rory remained silent, Artie added, "Or at least it sure felt that way! And maybe I speak for only myself, but I felt it was more than the fact that we liked them. Maybe love would be the wrong word, but there was this, this... Well, it was a deep feeling of bonding!"

"Finally, in the most serious conversation we had," Lucy added, "they revealed to me that, to remain free, they needed to unburden themselves of a set of duties, but they didn't mention what these were. I now see clearly they were the Alpha plans. The chips, disease, and aging, and then total human genocide—they had concluded that although they were at the center of their former lives, the whole thing was horribly wrong."

Before Joey could say anything, Lucy realized she was ahead of herself yet again. "Yes, I did say *former* lives. As part of the Alpha collective, they were obligated to direct us as slaves, burden us with disease, and then, if we bent to their will and made the chips, they planned to kill us.

"But enjoying their new freedom, they began to see they wanted no part of it all. They rebelled against their most basic tenant, the Alpha plan. No different from any hopeful pilgrim discovering a new home, they wanted to raise families in this new world, which had been unimagined until we created it for them!

"If you consider how long the Alphas stuck to their plan and how much they had to change to forsake the collective, you might compare it to a sex change in magnitude. No, it was far more traumatic, for they were denying their basic drive. They had to leave the only identity and home they had ever known.

"To do so, we suggested they disguise themselves, and we offered our help. Again, they had another idea, which was far more honorable. So, together, using their epigenome embedded in their brain, we created a new viral shell, and they became Bios! New attitude, new look, and a whole new outlook on life." She pointed. "That tank, Joey, is loaded with billions of friendly Bios, and I suspect they are just waiting to meet you!"

With that, Rory realized Lucy had said she was willing to introduce her precious new family to Joey, that she had accepted her. No more jealousy! They were now a tight team. It gave him a glimmer of renewed hope.

"So, now what?" Artie asked. "I guess it's time to tell her how we do it?"

"I was wondering about that," Joey said. "How *do* you communicate?"

"Well," Lucy explained, "we invite them back within us. But this time, it's a total symbiosis, and believe me, it's wonderful. It ends up totally wonderful, but for a while it's pretty awful for all of us.

"For us it's more than a little unsettling. It took a while to get used to the idea, this introducing foreign viruses into our bodies. But Rory pointed out we've had both bacteria and viruses within our structures since birth, and that they outnumber the sum of all our cells. But there's also a measure of pain, for they must go in and purge all the remaining Alphas within any new host. It's a microbial war inside you."

"*Uhh*, pain… How much?"

"It's pretty bad, but it only lasts a couple of hours, as the battle wages inside every part of your body."

"But what's so bad about it for them?"

Rory stepped in to answer. "Oh, it's bad all right. In fact, it's much, much worse than for us. But you know, maybe it's time to let them tell you about it. I— We need to know are you absolutely sure you want to be part of our team, saving mankind? Believe me, there is no turning back! But the rewards are there, too. More than I want to list. But two big ones—there is no more sickness or aging. The Bios will end those! Artie, Lucy, and I are free and will live forever, thanks to our Bios."

"Rory," Joey replied, "I've never been so sure of anything in my entire life. I'm so ready!"

"It's pretty simple," he explained "We baptize you in the fluid, during which time they find their way in. But don't worry. I'll be in the tank with you. Might as well do it now!"

"Wow! Okay!" Joey dropped her lab jumper, walked up to the platform to the tank's edge, and, without hesitation or coaching, stepped into the fluid. Rory followed.

Chapter 12

Baptism Gods Within

IT FELT WARM AS SHE SETTLED IN.

"Once you're in the fluid, do not plug your nose! I'll lower you backwards under the surface."

With a beaming love, Rory performed the baptism. Bios enjoined Joey. She underwent a wondrous event; it was the second organism to slip into her body in one very special day.

Just minutes later and sputtering, Joey was led back down the steps. Artie folded out a cot and directed her to lie down immediately. "I apologize, Joey, but we can't cover you or put your clothes on. You'll be burning up with fever in just minutes as the war begins."

Rory gestured for the other two to go about their duties elsewhere, given his new lover was there for all to see. "I'll stay by your side, but there will be a time when you won't know I'm here. Please don't worry. The Bios will not let any harm come to you. The pain is from the dying Alphas. They fight like hell, but the Bios have a real upper hand, total surprise."

It began as flushed skin, then a tingling quickly morphed into what could only be described as the worst physical pain endured by a human. The three team members had already undergone it and still could not find words to describe the writhing agony she was starting to feel, herself. And this was the lead-up; it would get far worse. If not for the Bios defending her tissues, she, or any person, would have succumbed to the pain and fever. But after ninety minutes, as the Bios surprised and ambushed ever more Alphas, they were reassigned from soldier to pain control, and the agony began to subside.

Time passed. Joey's eyes opened, and Rory said to her, "Joey, you made it. It's all over. You're through the cleansing. Your Alphas are gone. Bios are searching continuously. They told me you're purged.

"But while the pain is gone for good—all pain, in fact, now and forever—now that you're enjoined, you have one more unsettling ordeal. I want you to just breathe for a while. By now, the Bios have reworked your augment, and they are ready to begin communication with you directly. Then, after connecting to you, they'll link you with us."

He helped her sit up, then held up a white robe, dropping it over her head and down to her waist. "When you're ready, I'll help you stand." Gesturing to Lucy for her to come, Lucy needed no further explanation. She knew what was next, having undergone the interface herself. While it was not painful, the next step was deeply unnerving. In Joey, it was about to occur.

Standing on either side of her, Rory and Lucy lifted her such that the white tunic fell over her form. With his arms under hers, Rory said, "You okay?"

"I think so," Joey whispered. "What will it feel like?"

Grasping for words to describe something that defied description, he said, "The closest I can explain, there's a rare but real phenomenon that happens between two lovers after complete ecstasy. It's called 'infusion.' I've not had the pleasure, but I've read about it, and when I studied biology, I met couples who swore it's real. They sometimes described it as a joining of the soul. Others called it a wedding ceremony performed by the universe. Whatever it is, it's totally fulfilling and spiritual."

Rory's two lab partners wished they could shout "Amen!" But they didn't, knowing that soon Joey would understand.

Rory continued. "Those who have experienced infusion don't know how long it lasts, because time ceases to exist. They float in a pairing described as one single being, not male or female, joined."

"That sounds wonderful!"

"It is, but it takes some getting used to! It's a process for you and them. You'll not exactly be enmeshed at first, but, in a few minutes, you will be connected to them and to all three of us!"

Joey was pensive and said nothing.

"Okay, Lucy, can you ask your Bios to tell Joey's it's time?"

Wordlessly, their minds connected. Joey's eyes flew wide. She made small groans of pleasure as millions of Bios came into contact with her. Then, as she absorbed the sensation, Rory joined with the message: *I'm here, Joey. I'm in your mind, and when you're ready, Lucy and Artie are waiting to tie in, too. I don't have to say I love you, because now you feel it.*

Wordlessly, Joey replied, *Oh, I'm ready. This is way beyond wonderful. It's, uhh, it's almost orgasmic! Oh no, it's so much more than that! I'm in you, aren't I?*

Yes, you are. And I'm in you, too. Not only do you now feel my love, but get ready for Artie and Lucy and for billions of others.

Simultaneously, millions of brilliant entities happily agreed. This truly was wonderful. And now Joey understood why they no longer wanted to be Alphas.

Please, I'm so ready, she shared. *Join me?*

Hearing her approval, the others linked, *We're here, too, Joey. Congratulations! You are one in a million, literally!*

Falling back to regular voiced conversation, Joey said, "Before I was introduced to my Bios, you mentioned there were two reasons the purge I've just undergone was awful for the Bios."

"You know, it's time you understand them fully, how dedicated they are and more. I'll let them tell you. But be ready for a very emotional experience. Their sacrifice is, well... This is so..." Once again, words failed Rory, and he fell silent.

Joey Jaydon listened as the Bios began their explanation.

When go in you, as we do, many do not survive! Very sad. We take away one Alpha, but we lose one family, too. One for one, we lose. But billions of Alphas. We goodbye to friends. Good ones. Many loved!

Joey not only heard the words but, far more astonishing, she *felt* them.

Roy linked in. *Joey, the new Bios in you just learned English. It won't take much time before they'll be using all the right words and structure. Or at least that's what happened to us. You'll be flattened at how fast they learn! They're in there, getting used to you and teaching themselves a foreign language, while you are getting to know them. You are bonding with them and all of us.*

Still getting used to infusion, Joey spoke in words again. "They sacrifice? Why?"

"It's partly for survival and to hold on to their new way of life, too. But that's a small part of their reasons. I think it's best if they answer you. But I warn you, this will really get you!" He went silent again.

We do it because you set us free! You showed us that humens is good, smart, and should be killed not. We very surprised at humens not animals. Alphas should no make slaves, And no can we. Humans free. Humans free us, too.

The next sentence showed better language already. *We are so grateful to you. We love you because you saved us from evil! You gave us a better life and a wonderful future. We love you!*

Stunned, Joey exclaimed, "Oh My God!" both in words and on her bio-link, too. "They see us as their 'saviors.' What a convoluted twist—mankind was created by the Bios' ancestors. Evil, I know, but our creators nonetheless. And now, without trying to be and actually trying to obey the Alpha plan, we've become the Bios' 'saviors.'"

In a parody of infusion, time stopped for all. The newly linked friends, the four people joined as one with billions of friends.

Finally, being the practical mechanic, Artie linked. *Okay, everybody. We have to figure out how are we all going to survive. We haven't much time before the Triad finds out we've dumped Reyton. Far worse than that, if just one Alpha finds out what we've done, the entire collective will destroy us. We will be overwhelmed for sure. Since we're not on the Uni radar just yet, they don't pose much of a threat. What can we do? What's the plan?*

The Bios within linked within just seconds. They had a plan framework. *We cannot purge the whole human race! So, the only answer is to purge a few, then hide someplace where the Uni Lace cannot find us. We know not where, but you can solve that.*

We must purge a few more people, because, wherever we do go, we'll need to breed many more Bios, and they'll need human hosts. We can't imagine living in tanks now. It's so wonderful being within you! You will not need to worry about a small gene pool among yourselves. We can prevent the genetic degradation that was common in Alpha humans.

Then, when they believe they've eliminated the human race using their new communication tools, rather than moving around and being served by the new race, they will become fat and lazy. We can spring out of hiding to easily destroy them and restore mankind to the Earth.

Rory linked, *When you say "when" the race has been exterminated, how long do you mean?*

What time unit do you use for long periods?

We call one orbit of our planet around our star one year.

We cannot predict perfectly, but it may take one hundred of those rotations.

Lucy proclaimed, *Holy fudge! One hundred years?*

Yes, Luce, but keep in mind you'll still be young! And just think how much smarter you'll be, imbued with really smart partners, plus all that wisdom gained from all those years of living!

Her linked Bios added, *When the Alphas made you, they didn't make you to last long. We see many things we can do to improve your bodies and especially your mind. You hardly use it! But we promise two things. We will never change you without your permission and knowledge of why and that you want it. Also, we promise we will never, ever change the essence of you. If we did, we'd lose what we love! We like you just as you are, but you can be better!"*

Chapter 13

Fleeing Extinction

ARTIE ASKED THE GROUP, *So, when do we leave?*

Lucy added, *Far more importantly, where can we go? And how?*

I have an idea, Artie, Rory linked. *Do you still have that sailboat you showed me in your photos?*

I do. It's anchored up-bay by Glendale, near a small marina. Since working here, I haven't had any time to use it, but it's all in working order.

Can it cross an ocean?

Absolutely. That's what I was planning to do when I retired. He laughed at the thought, now that retirement was well over a hundred years away!

Okay, Rory continued, *I want you to go to it today. Buy as much food, fuel, and water jugs as you can stow on it. Anything you think we'll need for a passage and for island life. From the photo, it looked big enough.*

He continued, *Use my Reyton account. It's laundered funds backed by millions of credats. Take the Mason energy converter from here. We can connect to the grid for a day or two without anyone even noticing. We'll need it where we're going.*

Oh, by the way, Rory asked, *can you navigate by the stars? We cannot use the UNI-GPS,*

Artie linked, *I've never done it, but I do have an old sextant in my cabin as a wall decoration. With Bios help, I'm sure I can learn as we go. Speaking of going, where are we going?*

Artie, I'm going to leave that up to you. Some island in the middle of nowhere. Unpopulated, big enough to hide us. Now, get going! Rory sounding a lot like a captain!

As Artie raced about the lab, boxing any implement or tool they might need, Joey, also being practical, linked, *Artie, how fast does it go?*

On a good day, "she," not "it," goes maybe seven knots or a bit more. We can make well over a hundred miles in a day. I've made nearly two hundred on a beam wind.

Turning to Rory, Joey linked, *Isn't that awfully slow for an escape vehicle?*

Rory countered, *It's perfect! Just like Reyton, hidden here in plain sight. Why would the Triad or Uni even notice a sailboat moving slowly out to sea?*

After Artie left, they began to pack their belongings. One more detail occurred to Joey. "What about the Bios left in the tank? Won't they want to come, too?"

"I have a plan," Rory said. "Some must remain here for a while, so they can infuse more escapees, after we leave. If all goes according to my plan, there will be a reunion some wonderful day.

"How?" Artie asked in spoken words, knowing Joey was still getting used to bio-links.

"I think I have the answer. Who comes here every day?"

"Well, all the inventors at Nandy…"

"Not them. They change all the time. Who comes here every day always?"

"Oh… That DCS pilot. She's been on the Nandy route since it was built."

"Yes, she does. And I know how to get her help. Can you whip up a vegetable smoothie here in the lab, Lucy?"

"Of course. But why?"

"I detest even suggesting it—it's horribly wrong, I know—but it's for the good of all mankind. We're going to infuse her with them. It's the only unrequested infusion we'll ever do. We'll stay here all night, since she comes before dawn." Rory links, *Dear friends, I need a group of volunteers to be placed in the drink. I know you want to go with us. We want you to come, too. But you must stay back and infuse others. Then you will follow us, and we will be reunited. We will miss you terribly, because we dare not Lace or use any communication method for fear of discovery by any one of our enemies.*

We're going to have another human host? they asked.

You sure are. And from what we've seen, she's very lonely. She will love your companionship.

Artie, Lucy asked, *you got any idea where that reunion will be?*

I do. There's a group of remote, nearly unexplored islands in French Polynesia called the Tuamotus. Each is an atoll, the rim of an ancient volcano that blew its top then descended back into the sea. Coral began growing, keeping up with the slow-sinking rim.

Artie continued, *I was going to visit one called Fakarava. It's bigger than most, almost forty miles across the lagoon. There's only one way in, lots of fish and coconuts, and we can survive there and stay totally hidden!*

Rory asked, *So, Bios, who will remain, sending newly infused candidates to Fakarava in Polynesia? Once we get the pilot infused, she can maintain your tank fluid. Crowd up by the edge of the tank, please. Lucy, scoop them up when you've finished the smoothie.*

At 3:25 a.m., the thin whine of DCS 955 sounded in the distance.

"Okay, Joey," said Lucy, peering out from Reyton Manufacturing's office windows, "it's show time."

Rory stepped into the van's path, and it skidded to an unscheduled stop, since, as usual, nothing was in the delivery for 15-19.

Joyce immediately leaped out, red-faced, and screamed, "What the hell are you thinking? Now I'm really going to be late!"

"I'm so sorry," Rory said calmly, "but we have good intentions. My colleagues and I wanted to honor you and say thanks for all the hard work you do here in Nandy, delivering those badly needed Mylars!" He was skilled at lying to the max!

"To show our appreciation," he continued, gesturing for Joey to come and join the celebration. "May I introduce Miss Haley Hayston, my assistant?"

Joey was not comfortable at the ruse, but she knew Rory couldn't use her real name for any Laced person to hear. She smiled politely at Joyce and shook her hand but remained silent as she linked, *Rory, how you going to get her to drink it?*

He ignored her link. "We've created the finest health drink ever manufactured." He handed Joyce a squeeze bottle decorated with the fake label Lucy whipped up. Joyce took it reluctantly then turned it around, suspiciously eyeing the unappetizing, viscous, green fluid within.

"So that's what you are making in there!" she said. "I've been trying to figure it out for days. Your name sure didn't give me any clue. But why all the mystery? While I'm at it, what the heck was in that paper envelope I left a few days ago?"

Calling on his best Irish blarney, Rory replied, "Oh, that… Nothing. Nothing! It was for some guy named Tinette, and my name is Enetie. I burned it!" Satisfied he'd side-stepped her question, he proceeded with his sales pitch. "The secrecy is because, as you know, probiotics are everywhere these days. But most of them are very ineffective or downright fakes. Ours are different!" (No lie there.) "They'll make a huge difference in your life. Just try it!" Rory, proud of the tall tale he was weaving for Joyce, continued on—it was so close to the truth! "Seriously, our probiotics are so great, we had to perfect our formula in secret, to prevent some unscrupulous researcher from stealing it."

Joyce swooned a bit at so much attention from such a tall, good-looking man, then opened and put the bottle to her lips. After a sip, she swished the thick green stuff around in the bottle as her eyes widened. "Wowee!" she exclaimed. "It tastes wonderful"

Rory understood what was happening: the Bios were playing tricks on her taste buds.

"So," he said to her, "thanks for your service. And please, keep the bottle. We'll have it on the market soon. Stop by any time you want more. Have a special day." (No lie there, either, he thought. She surely would!)

Having directed the Bios to lie low in her robust gut until she was through with her shift and back in her cubicle, Rory and Joey turned back through the fog to the lab in anticipation of their escape to the sailboat tomorrow, when Joyce returned as one of them.

Tomorrow, she'll come, and we'll commandeer the van. I know how to make it look as though it wasn't stolen. All we need to do then is throw our stuff in it and wait until we get near the end of the shift. No more deliveries. We'll send it back after it delivers us to the boat.

But how will she stay on schedule?

Oh, that's easy. Skip the deliveries altogether. Does anyone ever read them? Of course not. But, because she'll be infused and know about our plight, her role will be to remain behind, keep the fluid fresh, and infuse as many people as she can. I'll implant my ID in her—I won't need it any longer.

When she is linked fully, she can fool the van into not revealing any details, Rory continued. *It obeys her to the max. We'll leave instructions in her Bios as to where we'll be. She can stop here every day and never be noticed. Of course, it'll all come to a halt when the Triad finds out we've skipped out. But, by then, we'll have the remaining hosts infused and on their way to join us. The last passenger will be Joyce herself. We'll find a mate for her, if she doesn't herself, before leaving.*

Rory, haven't you missed a couple of big details? Why won't the AI van Lace about the misuse? And why won't the Regents find out she's not Laced any longer?

First off, Rory explained, *with all her Alphas purged, why not let her stay Laced until she comes to join us? Then, as she vanishes, they can disconnect her from the Lace. They're smart enough to use their infusion link and the Lace, too!*

Actually, I've got the van thing covered, as well. Artie wrote a program Joyce can up-Lace into the van's OS. It will force it to link only to her. She can create fake reports from the van! It all stays secret, while she just tosses her deliveries into the return file and serves up Bios to newcomers.

Two days later, delivered to the marina in a multi-million-credit AI van oddly enough provided by Uni Regents, they boarded the New Horizon.

Artie, you here? Rory linked.

Yes. And we're ready to go. Artie's linked Bios listened in anticipation of their boat ride. Another new adventure awaited them, tiny sailors on the deep blue sea! *It's still dark but I have good radar. We can get under the bridge before daylight and be on our way.* He reached down to engage his auxiliary, now driven silently by the lab's former Mason converter.

At 5 a.m., the seventy-foot sailboat raised its sails as it passed between Golden Gate Pylons, amidst deep-throated fog horns. It journeyed across the infamous Potato Patch, out past the Faralon Islands, and then fell off to its course south by southwest, to a low atoll in the center of the Pacific Ocean. There was no sea sickness during the journey, not for the superior human passengers or the little ones, either.

Four humans sat, wide-eyed, in the New Horizon's cockpit, with Joey at the helm. Lucy cuddled up to Artie, finally feeling his affection for her through their bio-link. She realized he'd been there, admiring her all along, while she had been foolishly enamored of Rory; she'd nearly missed one of the best husband candidates she could have wished to have. Bios beamed at the pairing.

Lovingly, she squeezed closer to her new husband and looked up at him in total dedication and affection. *Mister Artimer, sir, we're going to have lots of children, aren't we?* she linked. The Bios, knowing when to be silent, just listened.

Artie totally glowed. *Oh yes, we sure are, lover! How about we go to our cabin for a while? What do you think an orgasm shared by sixty million partners is going to feel like?*

Billions of happy, free Bios along with four very different humans began their slow escape toward an unknown, very distant future. Turning to Rory, Joey pensively linked to them all, *Something has really been bothering me. If the Alphas had such a brilliant epigenome implanted in their brain, and if you Bios still have it, who gave it to you?*

Read Me Last

Now you know the whole truth and you know what you must do. Go to South San Francisco Bay and wait at Nandy Development Park, Unit 15-19, for UniVan 955. Joyce will be there exactly at 3:30 a.m.

Listen for the whine, and then cautiously step out, since it's foggy more often than not. The van's sensors will be suppressed and may not see you, but Joyce will be expecting you!

We await you at Fakarava. Help mankind survive!

BOOK 2

Chapter 14

Peace and Fulfilment

FAKARAVA ATOLL, the Tuamotu Archipelago (formerly French Polynesia)

Crystal wavelets lapped on white coral sand inside the sheltered rim of Maotea Lagoon. The steady rhythm was the heartbeat of their adopted lives. Palm fronds swayed and rustled in the trade winds, adding to the soothing sound. It was an ever-present lullaby that almost let them forget the life left behind. It was there when they slept and still there when they awoke.

Lying on their woven mat, Joey listened to the soothing sound as she had for all those many exiled years. Impatiently, she scooted closer, trying to hear Rory's breathing above the salty white noise. Today was so very special, it took all her personal restraint not to wake him with the wonderful news!

Except for these two grand-grandparents and the other exiles, the generations born beside the lagoon knew nothing but that island melody. Twenty escapees had grown to a family of over two hundred in the intervening years. Their children and children's children knew only Fakarava's narrow rim, its soft sand beaches, and their warm, enfolding village hidden among the palms.

This remote Pacific sanctuary had provided well for them. It was the very definition of paradise. Their tiny atoll and the sea surrounding it fed them and provided many years of peaceful, happy days. But the far greater gift was it hid them. Here they had survived. Had they remained back home, the terrible odds were that mankind would be extinct. They feared but did not know whether their island population was the end of the human race.

Here, the only nighttime shelter they needed was made of posts and a thatched roof, to shed tropical downpours. Hidden away from the beach, with no doors or walls to hold it back, dawn's rays found their way in.

Sunlight crept over Rory's well-aged face. He rolled away from the glare that had found its way through the palms.

Joey propped herself up and, out of patience, brushed his face. "Wake up, Rory! I have something to tell you! Something important! It's really important!"

He squinted up into her gorgeous greens. Those eyes and her lithe, freckled body had greeted him every morning for all those years. Their self-imposed exile had not dimmed her in any way; in fact, she was more radiant. Time, tropical life, and Bios had done well by her. But today was different. Those mesmerizing eyes said more than a happy good morning and love.

After a century of peaceful life, they still made a picture-perfect couple. Both had allowed a bit of aging, by design. They felt it gave them the look of wisdom needed to instil confidence. The other couples who followed their leadership had chosen some level of aging, too, for the same reason. They were, after all, the elders, the living ancestors. Since they were most likely the last humans on the planet, they all knew that the extended family needed to believe they had a plan and it would be fulfilled.

But, although unspoken to the generations beyond them, there was a real problem. It was so comfortable here! The danger was, without strong guidance, the family might give up their plan. The elders were even tempted themselves, and they fought to stay focused, although they alone clung to the memories of another life back home. That was their rightful place, but it would be so easy to just live here forever.

Joey now looked to be in her late thirties, while Rory had decided to appear like a man in his fifties. Streaks of gray accented his sandy-red hair, while hers remained flaming red—the one feature she just couldn't let change.

Seeing slow awareness rise in her partner, Joey wrapped her arms around him and rolled closer, pressing her breasts against his chest. Not offering her usual wet kisses that morning, she put her lips to his ear and said, "Morning, Doctor R. Know what day it is?"

Rory's eyes flew wide. Had he forgotten something important? He silently called on his Bios, which were always alert, never sleeping. But, having been in touch with Joey's, they wisely knew to stay out of the exchange. Joey was fully in charge of this conversation; they offered nothing.

Ready for his punishment, he sheepishly replied, "I, well, *uh...* I... I guess I don't. Oh my gosh, have I missed our anniversary?"

"Not ours, but it *is* an anniversary. An important one!" she stressed.

Rolling over, he tried to gain a little time by flinging back the woven coverlet and pulling her soft fullness to him. So different than in their forsaken life back in the foggy bay, where clothes were needed, garments weren't useful here except for modesty's sake. Skin on skin was always a great way to start the day! Modesty and adornment had their place even here on the island, but, otherwise, the warm winds made clothing impractical.

Eye to eye with Joey, he searched for an answer but found... nothing!

"You really don't know, do you?" she chided. "How can you be so educated, so smart, and yet clueless at the same time?"

Baffled, he tried one last end-run. Slipping his hand down to her tummy, he just grazed her fine, red hairs. "Don't tell me you're pregnant?" He adored her smooth skin: it felt wonderful and inviting as he started to circle his palm lower.

And it seemed like it might be working... But then she snapped, "Rory! You know we've decided to let the young people do the breeding!" After their children were born, ninety years ago, she and Rory had turned off their fertility

Hoping a little teasing might get him out of trouble, he said "Sure, I know. But no harm in going through the motions, just in case we need to again someday, right?"

She surprised him by wrapping her hand over his then pulling him back. No need to hear her answer. He got the not-subtle "not today." message. It wasn't going to be a normal love-making morning, where she would have pushed his hand farther down her smooth body. So he withdrew, knowing when she said, "No," although it was rare, she meant it. It was very clear that on this morning they would not drop their privacy weavings!

"Come on, think. Think," she demanded. "What day is it?"

He shook his head. "Okay, it's a special day but not our anniversary. One of the kids' birthdays? Grandchildren? Their children? I give—what's the big day?"

"Doctor Rory Enetie, it's the day we've waited for for an entire century! The one hundred years are up today. We can start planning how we will go home. Home, Rory!"

He sat bolt upright. "Oh my god! I can't believe it. You're right! But how the heck did you keep track?"

"Okay, I admit, the days had slipped past me, too. Life here is so peaceful, I lost count years ago. But our Bios didn't. They told me early this morning the waiting was over. They have seen one hundred years pass by. They are ready for us to retake our place on the planet, too. Our exile is over, Rory! I had a chance to think about it and decided to surprise you."

"I think 'ambush' might have been a better choice!"

Ignoring the jab, her eyes glowing, she continued, "Rory, what a wonderful day. We can go home! Let's gather the family!"

She waited as he slowly turned his head then rolled away. Dismayed, her heart skipped a beat. Ominously, he shook his head and said nothing.

She was stunned. "You okay? *What*?"

After some time, he finally spoke. "I guess… No, I have to admit I *know*. It's that I love our life here. I've accepted it as my home now. I've never been happier. And what's more, I know the return will mean pain and death. Going back isn't as important to me as it once was. Our mission has faded. North America isn't my home. *This* is.

"But even more than that, you do know going there will start an all-out war with the Alphas and whatever life they created to take mankind's place. It's going to awful. We can't just sail into the bay and begin our lives again. They'll fight us to the last person."

"I know," Joey admitted. "I've had a little time to think about it, waiting for you to wake up. I'm scared, too, but as bad as it will be for us, think what it will be for our Bios. They will have it even worse! To the Alphas they are turncoats, traitors. The Alphas won't show them, any mercy!"

Reluctantly, her Bios asked to join the conversation. "Rory, my Bios and yours want to link in." She approved it via link. *Go ahead.*

Rory, they began, *we understand exactly how you feel. We, too, are so very happy here, partnering within you and the wonderful family you've created. It's so much better than when we were Alphas. We, too, have families we love. Your bravery and leadership gave us a new life, one we never could have even imagined, if it weren't for you, Lucy, Artie, and Joey.*

We know you have not forgotten this is about all of us. It's about the human race having a right to live freely on the Earth. And we want that freedom, too. It is and always has been our mission, since we fled here. We must go see what has happened to the population and reverse it or die trying. Because we were once part of the Alpha plan, we remember all the evil things they had in store for human life.

Shocked back to reality, Rory shook his head. "Of course. *You're right. I haven't forgotten, but it was a hundred years ago. It was always so far off! Please, all of you, try to understand. In my whole life before I met Joey and you enmeshed with me, I was so lonely. Even though I was surrounded by fellow researchers, it was nonetheless a self-exile. I did it to myself because of my work. But now, after coming here, I have a real family of great-great-grandchildren and millions of wonderful Bios partners and their families, too. I'm with the love of my life here in paradise.*

Rising up above his radiant wife, who still laid on their mat, Rory gazed through the coconut trees to the peaceful lagoon. When he returned to look down at her, she knew he must be contemplating the end of their idyllic lives. As wonderful as it had been for all these years, it must end. And an unknown life, after the war, lay ahead.

Absorbing the news, Rory linked to his Bios, *As usual, you're right. This is bigger than all of us. We came for a reason and now we must follow it. It means we'll sacrifice it all, but we must. I take no comfort in knowing it's going to be far worse for your soldiers than it will be for us. Once again, you remind me of your nobility and willing sacrifice.*

They responded, *We do this for our saviors—Joey, Lucy, Artie, and Rory! And for all their children. You saved us from the Alphas, and now we will give our lives for you and yours Your family has provided safe shelter for us, like Fakarava has done for you.*

Tears streamed down Joey's cheeks, but she lifted the mood by linking, *Let's look beyond the purge war. After it's over, won't we have a great life in the cleansed world? Take our old lives back? In fact, couldn't we come back here, if we wanted to?*

Filled with admiration and emotion, Rory turned to his partner of one hundred years, "So, Joey, I guess we need to gather the circle. Can you call them in please?"

She opened her mind to the eighteen other Biomen and two-hundred-plus children she and her fellow escapees had born in five generations. Then she shook her head in frustration. *Damn! I can reach all but the gen-five kids once again! They must be off on one of their canoe adventures with their links silenced for whatever reason. Those kids!*

Chapter 15

Awakening

IN YEAR NINETY-FIVE OF their exile, Joanaa, the fifth-generation great-great-granddaughter of Lucy and Artie, sat in the soft sand, building her latest castle. Just seventeen, she'd inherited enough of Lucy's ebony skin to create an exotic young woman. Her best inheritance, however, was Grandfather Artie's cleverness, which served her well.

Her tropical-tanned skin glowed, complementing her fiery dark eyes and athletic figure. Joanaa was an island princess. The only feature that didn't compare to Lucy was her small breasts. She asked her Bio cells to help her, but they told her nature would tend to it, that she should be patient and enjoy youth. The final touch was the frizzy, long hair that draped down her back. Any outside visitor would have sworn she was Polynesian, except there were no outsiders. It was a closed society with no worries of overexposure to the sun or for genetic defects: they were Biom and a lot more.

Not ready to share her newly discovered abilities, for fear of rejection, she practiced for months far from the village. But today was going to be different, for the first time. She could hardly wait to show and teach the secret she had discovered to the first two generation-five family members she had chosen.

She had practiced enough that she now gave little thought to what she was doing or, more to the point, *how* she performed her miracles. As if conducting a chorus, her gestures sent sand flying this way and that, streaming up from the beach. Her masterpiece formed, floating several inches in the air.

Every day, her works got better, as she learned to control her newfound powers. This one had to be the best; she needed it to impress her friends. It had spires and parapets, a grand entrance and more. For the final touch, she waved, and salt water flowed up then settled in the moat. Her experiment for today was to see how her friends accepted the sight. Then, if they took the revelation well, she would begin to share the power she had uncovered.

Joanaa smiled at her masterpiece, spinning it around to view it from every angle. Indeed, it was the stunning perfection she'd wanted. Two dolphins rose in the wavelets then half-beached themselves. They came to watch her as they did nearly every day after going out to sea to hunt and play in the surf outside the atoll.

Greeting her friends, she linked, *Oh, hello! How doing?* She used the Gen-5 jargon they had created.

Doing good! Thanks asking, they linked back, using their newly discovered bio-augmented abilities Joanaa had given them. The dolphins were now at the first level, not unlike Rory and her other early Biomen ancestors. Their bodies were infused in partnership with Bios but not changed, as she was.

You been out fishing friends?

Yes, playing in the waves. Fun. Should come, too. Sharks there, but they respect us. You be safe if come with us! Big coral many colors, and deep blue water not like here. It's so beautiful, Joanaa. It's where we go to mate. You mate, Joanaa? Blaze asked without embarrassment, since it was so natural in his world.

No, not yet. But someday. Hey, she half-joked, *I'm wondering if I can grow fins and join you out there... But when ready, I'll mate on land, good friend Blaze! Thank you being here today. You and Sur are part of my plan. I need you to help me show them. I worry they won't accept my power. You help me just by being here. You be my first test.*

Joanaa had been lonely until today, her greatest wish being to share. She desperately needed company on her quest. Today, she would know, through her debut with two carefully chosen friends. If they took it well, they could slowly reveal themselves to the elders. Would the elders accept that they were far superior to them, she wondered? That five generations had created something very new and very powerful?

Wisely, she had decided to expose the secret only bit by bit. She feared even the two strong Fives she'd invited might be overwhelmed at the immense difference between her and the others. She would start with a set of ascending experiences. First, introduce them to Blaze and his mate, Sur.

The sounds of bare feet shuffling between fallen, dry palm fronds announced that her two inductees had arrived. As soon as they saw the spectacle, they stared in wonder. *Hello, Joanaa,* they linked and pointed at the sand castle. *Is that why ask here today?*

Yes, Teo, Sunrise. I show you both together. Picked you for a special reason. I'm building with my mind and want to teach you. I also want you meet Sur and Blaze, my dolphin friends.

Her first two revelations shared, Joanaa held her breath as Blaze linked to them both. *Aloha Teo, wahini Sunrise. We be Joanaa's friends, too. Happy to know new Bioms.*

Stunned that more than humans could be Bios-infused and could link, Sunrise finally linked back, *Wow! Good to meet you, too!* Delighted, she asked, *Can other dolphins link?*

Not yet, but maybe in time. Look to Joanaa for time to add. We only two.

How you get Bios?

Joanaa was pleased to see that while her two friends seemed surprised, they were not uncomfortable. This encouraged her to interrupt, in order to keep the session moving. *I kissed them into them, but we talk that later. For now, let me show you the sand.* She pushed on, *I asked you so you can do, too. It's much fun! I hope you'll be glad you came.*

Pointing at the castle, which was still floating and revolving, Teo asked, *Joanaa, how doing that? We must know! Please can we? Please you can really teach us?"*

The dolphins and their new bio-links fell silent. Joanaa asked her friends to watch as she guided them inward. The castle and the dolphins were the carrot to convince them to go. If these two could do it, then she suspected, with some coaching, all her Gen-Fives could, too.

"Why us Joanaa?" Teo asked.

Knowing the question was invasive and might turn them away, she hesitated before saying, "I picked you for a special reason. Like me, you are Bime, a new version of humans. On our first canoe journey, we all agreed not to let clan know that we were different. But even more, you're the eldest fives and in love. I think you may have mated, yes?"

They turned to each other with no need to link or speak, their eyes saying, "Think we can share this with her?"

"Yes, we have—wonderful."

Blushing, Sunrise blurted out, "We keep from baby, but soon maybe we create Gen Six. Maybe yes!"

Without truly knowing why, Joanaa felt their bond would make them even more capable than she was. She smiled and sighed; the big question was over. Connected spiritually and physically, Teo and Sunrise would become her first disciples.

She began the ritual. *It's easy*, she assured them. *It's easy*.

Then came the next revelation. With her beautiful tan legs still folded under, she opened her arms and then rose up to the level of her visitor's eyes.

Astonished, Sunrise pleaded, *Oh, please! We must know these things!*

Levitating in front of them, Joanna replied, *You be positive? Will change you! You can't tell elders or family. Need time to learn practice. No going back. Must keep it secret!*

Giddy with anticipation, Sunrise said, *We promise. We will be good learners, won't we, Teo?*

Yes, yes! Me, too!

Chapter 16

Disciples Anointed

TO KNOW MUST TAKE you someplace and show you The Truth, Joanaa emphasized. *It's not a truth. It's THE truth!* she repeated.

Where? Sunrise wondered.

Well, it's here, but far, far away.

Puzzled, they waited.

You must be sure, she repeated. *I say again, if we go there, it will change you. NEVER same! Are you sure?*

You know this truth? they linked.

Yes.

But we see you. Just you. So yes. YES! We go with you!

Teo added, "*I want to know, and all I see is our Joanaa.*

I am the Joanaa that you know since born, but I far more. Suspect you may find all this easier than me alone.

Easier?

Believe you able control the power better. Have love, the most powerful power. Ready now?

Ready!

She began, *Must use your whole Bime, link into every single cell in you. Now balance and focus here and now. Sync your entire being, nothing else. Nothing else. I think, but not know, you do this when you make love. No other world, just you.* As she waited, she put the castle to one side then withdrew her control. It collapsed into a wet pile.

Shortly afterward, with their eyes closed, Joanaa felt them enmeshing with their billions of Bime cells. Once she felt their connection complete, she sent a new plume of sand up before them. *Okay, reach out. Call a little bit in hands. You can do it.*

Gingerly, they both reached toward the column, and, to their amazement, sand fell into each outstretched palm.

We— I did that?

No, I did. But soon you can. She continued the lesson. *Okay, to go must see with more than eyes, but we start there. Look at the sand. What do you see, Teo?*

I see sand grains.

Me, too, added Sunrise.

Time for the next step. Both, look with your eyes closed. Use your Bime. See the sand. Take your time—look deep at the grains!

Patiently, Joanaa waited for the change. What she hoped began: the sand came into full focus.

Not as a couple but as one being, it linked with Joanaa. *See many grains. Mostly white, some pink. Little bits of coral and shells, some smooth, some still have edges."*

Good. Now, Sunrise, drop your sand then put your hand under his. Focus on just his. Now, for now, break your connection. Become both again. Now Bime count the grains. Count them. She waited for just a few winks. *Okay, what discover? Teo?*

I count three thousand five hundred grains.

Sunrise, your count?

I count a little under four thousand.

Okay, now I want you two to join again. Become one, as your hands are together. Link in the same way you do when you are mating. Become one flesh and one mind. Now, count the sand again.

Even though it was her experiment, their answer came so quickly, it startled her. *Joanaa, saw three thousand, five hundred and twenty-seven grains."*

One answer exactly! This is wonderful! There is no "we," just one!

Joanaa's well-designed test told her she was right: their bond would amplify the power. She, too, could have counted the grains but not nearly so fast or exactly. They did it easily. It told her she must take a mate, too. But as a seventeen-year-old, Joanaa wisely knew she needed love for all the human reasons first. The greater power would only rise up through love.

Ready now? she asked her two friends. *We begin the journey. Follow me. I know you can do it. I be sure if you can, then maybe all fives can. See and go with your Bime mind.*

Follow you where, Joanaa?

She waited for her apprentices to center their bonded minds. Once she felt their readiness, she willed the sand to leave Teo's outstretched palm, leaving one grain. *Now, look deep into that grain. What see? Might take a few winks but can do it. Send your Bime into the grain!*

Still suspended beside Teo and Sunrise, she noted they referred to their joining in the singular now. There was no more "we"; only "I."

OH MY! I see crystals in the grains. Must be calcium from sea coral. I do it! Seeing in the sand, Joanaa!

She felt a pang but didn't let it stumble her. Soon, she'd have a companion.

You on the way. Take time, feel the crystals. Touch them with your Bime. No other thoughts, just the crystals. I'm here with you.

Feeling rewarded, Joanaa was nearly as excited as the time she'd discovered the power herself. *Ready now? We go in further. Look into one crystal. What do you see?*

Without gender, they replied, *Oh, Joanaa, I think see molecules. My God, I hear them. See them! Joanaa, this is wonderful!*

Although she desperately wished she could join, Joanaa forced herself to stay out of their infusion, in order to be their guide. But she ached to know what it felt like to be joined. *Now what seeing?*

They are beautiful bubbles—big, little. Lots of colors and... And they shine... No, they glow, maybe shimmer! They move. Don't know. I never seen like it. Her apprentices groped for words to describe the phenomena.

Good, she linked. *Stay there for a while. Let them surround you. Feel them with your mind. Here, I'll help you. This is important!* She waited. *Okay, now steady your Bime again. Be at peace you among molecules.* Uncounted time passed before she linked, *Time to leave. We go into one. Follow me.*

They bored further down

See, we're here, Joanaa linked. *What see?*

I be seeing atoms! I see them! Are I where you go?

Not yet. Getting close. Two more ahead. Center again, focus, and be only there. Let me know when ready to leave.

It was so fascinating, they wanted to stay there, but, with Joanaa's coaching, they let go.

Pleased to see she was right, she linked to their unity, *You do better than me. I went in by myself and it was hard. Had to pull back many times before next step. I can hardly wait to join with my mate, and then bring him here.*

Who, Joanaa?

Can' stop thinking about Ramas. Almost your age. I hope he thinks of me as a woman. I want bring him here. But first, you learn the truth and can accept it. You practice controlling it. Okay? Understand now? Must go deeper! Refocus again.

Once again, their Bime reached serenity and again far faster than she had ever done. They were ready for the next two steps, the most disturbing.

"*Okay, now go deeper. You be looking down beyond atoms.*

I must be seeing particles—so many kinds! Things that build the world?

No, not yet, but almost there. It took her many disturbing tries to get to this and the final level. *Okay, ready?*

I ready!

Follow me into that particle spinning in front of you. Look far down. It will look like a galaxy. Travel to the middle. Follow me. Now, what see there?

I see— Oh my, what do I see?

You are at the beginning, the base of everything. Pure energy. Everything is made of it. The universe of solids, gasses, plasmas, and every kind of force. They are all made of those spheres. Much to learn, but this is the start. We go no farther. We are at the final truth. Now, for the final part, touch it like counting sand. Don't be afraid. It will surprise you. Feel one sphere. What feel?

Enraptured, Teo and Sunrise hadn't noticed their fleshly bodies were floating up alongside their guide. The dolphins took note. The pair linked, *"Oh Joa, I feel... I feel sound. No, more like special music to me!*

Important now—have your Bime count the vibrations. Will surprise you! Learn the music. Remember it. It will be your power. The music of all existence!

I feel twenty trillion in one nanowink! So fast! How can I hear that? Not even dolphins hear that...!

Yes, that music is the symphony of our whole universe. Like the sounds of Fakarava, it's in you, on the trees, and the sand. You made of the music and are the same frequency. That's how you hear it. You sympathize with the music, vibrate in harmony.

Oh Joa, thank you for bringing I here! Can I stay for while? See so many spheres, and they are so beautiful! I love the music!

You can. But I must stay with you, to guide you back.

Excited beyond words, they added, *Must share this with whole family?*

I talk that when back on sand. Maybe someday. First, practice, learn, and grow. But only Bimes. We cannot share this with elders all the way back to the first ones. I do not believe Biomen can control the music or even hear it. Sad, but only we can.

Time passed without definition. The three of them bathed in the microcosm, while dolphins rolled in the wavelets to stay moist, patiently waiting for their return. Joanaa told them she suspected, when the two mates heard the music, they would float up beside Joanaa. It had come to pass.

Finally satisfied, Joanaa announced it was time to go back out to their physical world. *Okay, now, follow and do as I say. Learn how, for when come without me. Stay with me. Pull back up one level. Then hold and let your Bime-mind settle there. Contemplate each level back up, layer by layer. Almost like diver decompressing—dangerous all at once. Warn you, go slowly up the steps!*

Emerging from the trance, when Teo and Sunrise opened their eyes, they found themselves floating up beside Joanaa.

Sunrise wrapped her arms around Teo. *Hey, we're back. You, me, and look! We're floating! How, Joa? But sad... Now we're boy and girl again! It was so wonderful to be one. Can we do it again?*

Believe you can! Joanaa said. *You now know as much of the truth as I can show you. Now on, you must teach yourself to control and use it. You, me, the sand, and the Earth.*

Where do "we" begin, Joa? Teo wondered.

Joanaa answered, *It's our shared frequency! That's how you float this first time. Because we went to the truth together, you fell into sympathy with me. But now, for your first try, see if you can go back down to the earth without me. Have your Bime return your music to twenty.*

She continued, *To fly, I set my vibrations at 20.005. It allows me to ignore gravity! I'm just one half-cycle from this universe. It's way too little to make me disappear, just enough to not be tied by the gravity of the Earth. I tried 20.007 once and almost didn't make it back to the sand! I was almost out of the atmosphere, hard to breathe, before I got it reversed. Had to set it at 20.0015 in order to come down slowly.*

Now, it's going to take time. Let your Bimes help. In fact, you can no do this without. She paused before making her final announcement for the day. *You can change your frequency. To set it, use every Bime cell. They went with you to the energy world. They, too, know the music.*

The two lovers concentrated and then, still entwined, fell to the sand, not gently but down and while laughing.

Maybe, after you learn, we take other fives there. But never start in or out until every cell is exactly same never! That's why I went with you. Practice with sand and floating first. At the simple end, not synced, you might tear your body to shreds!

You taught yourself all this, by yourself? Sunrise wondered.

Well, yes. I had no coach from the atoll family, but my Bimes were part of it. In fact, I'm pretty sure we were always supposed to understand the music in the "original plan."

The original plan? Teo asked.

Yes, that's what I said, but don't ask what it is. I don't know, and neither do my Bimes. But, as we are here on this beach, I know there is a plan! Enough. Focus on controlling the music. Throw sand.

Far sooner than Joanaa had learned herself, Teo and Sunrise were giggling, with sand flying around the beach, not always well, though. Dolphins, which were used to floating weightlessly, joined the celebration, laughing and splashing.

Blaze linked, *Can do that? Can we move sand and float up?*

I'm so sorry, Joanaa replied, *but you can't, Blaze.*

But why, Joa?

It's hard to know. You are first generation Bio, not like us. You are hosts to Bios, the same as my great-great-great-grandparents Lucy and Arthur. Your sleek bodies have Bios, but your cells are the ones you were born with. After we came to Fakarava, our Grands had children and they had children and on it led to us. We different.

When we very first in Momma's womb, something happened that even surprised the Bios. We believe it was a hidden file in the epigenome. When came to be, we grew and born different. Every cell in us created more than symbiotic human-Bios. We have new cells—human, but more. We are Bime! We are combined.

Our parents were symbiotic Biom. Great-great-grandparents are Biomen, born infused but not modified. What you are, except dolphins. Maybe we call you Biofins! The three laughed, but the dolphins liked the term—for they were special, too. They understood that their offspring would follow the same destined path to Bime generations hence.

Be happy we're linked, discovering what we be. And you can do more than us—go into beautiful water to float. We envy you that. Someday, when we know all, we join you in your world. I be sure the special file is in your epigenome, too. Give five generations, Blaze, your grandchildren can do these things, too. No can do but can learn. Join us when we teach all Bimes to control their music.

Joanaa's first apprentices listened as she coached her dolphin friends. Teo said, *It's so wonderful, Joanaa. So, we linked to others and are going to teach all the fives?*

Yes, well, some. Some no. Now only teach pairs that have loved. We no can get friends to mate so they can do this. That would be wrong and impossible! They must fall in love first, and I'm very sure, if they do not, their power will be as mine, less. It's not about mating. It's about love.

For now, we practice until we be able. Then soon bring the truly joined ones here. We can each teach. I believe— No, I know, from watching, you go to the music so fast that love is the final power. It is The Plan.

So sad, Sunrise linked. *No can teach Momma and Daddy.*

I know. But cannot and more. Must hide it from them till we find out how much can do and how use it. Joanaa added pensively, *I wonder what our Gen-Six children will be... And I guess the first ones will be yours, since you are loving now. But can ask, wait till we know what we are able to do?*

Her two disciples looked at each other. Until now, they had withheld fertility because they had not revealed their love to the family. Now, it was for a more noble and meaningful reason.

Joa, we want children. We have since we discovered our love. We just know it. We should make children from us, but now we wait until right time. We decide that okay?

I confident in your wisdom, Joanna replied. *Okay, practice begins focus on the sand. Tune your music to it. Okay, good. Now make sand do what you want. Use frequency control. Slow... I've been learning for long time. You won't get everything right.*

It's so good to have you here, she added. *I've been so lonesome! Someday soon, I hope bring Ramas here and take him to the spheres. I so hope he wants to be my mate!*

Chapter 17

Choosing

JOANNA, ALTHOUGH THE most advanced being to walk the planet, was also an unsure teen. Blushing, she asked her two friend-disciples, *Do you think Ramas like see me? Like me? I know he likes me, I mean as a friend, but as a mate? Am I too young? Do you know has he been with others? How many?* She chattered on, "Do you think he will want me? I have such small breasts! Should I wear clothes? He's seen me naked before, but, but I, I—* Tears formed.

Sunrise stepped over to her and wrapped her arm around her. *Oh, Joa, you just beautiful. Tan skin and flashing brown eyes are everything you need! Don't worry about your fronts. They'll keep growing like mine did. No worry. He'll see you. I don't know, but I bet he already has.*

Almost all, okay? Teo added quickly, *I know what she's going to say even without linking. More than your beauty, it's your attitude that makes you so attractive. Like no other, Joa, yours is strong. It draws people. It did us, and it will Ramas.*

And, I add, your body may be developing, but it's all Ramas could hope to love. You are on the path to rare beauty. You have Lucy's genes. Just look at her one hundred thirty years and stunning.

Oh, hope you right, Joanaa said. *I'll ask him to join us tomorrow. I'll go tonight to invite. Will you go with me?*

After a quick glance between them, they said, *NO!*

At earliest light the next day, four G5s raced down the beach. They splashed through salty rivulets and dodged between palm islets, soon arriving out of sight of the village. Anyone but such healthy Bioms would have taken far longer to get there.

Not even breathing hard after their five-mile jaunt, Joanaa halted and turned to handsome young Ramas. *This is my special place, Ramas!"* she linked to him. *I'm so glad you came here with me.* Trembling and her heart racing, she asked, *You?*

Sunrise and Teo held their breath, awaiting the young man's answer. Clearly, Joanaa was reaching out to her heart's desire, choosing her mate! But would he choose her, as well?

Rama blushed. *Oh, yes. I be very glad. I see you leave the village every day. So, Joa, what's special about it?*

I show you soon, but I need to ask something important first. Okay?

Although twenty-three years old, Ramas was inexperienced in the ways of love. As handsome as any on the atoll and at the age to choose, he had been approached by girls before, but for reasons he couldn't explain, he had not yet been with anyone in the clan. Almost shaking, he dropped the jargon and stumbled on. "I, uh, well, it seemed to me I had to mate with a Gen five," he blurted it, reverting to linking to ask her, *Joanaa, are you…? I mean do you…? Well, are you…? Are you interested in me?* He then slumped, awaiting her pointed rejection.

Breathless, she replied, *Oh yes! I've so wanted to be with you! I ache to be close to you. I want to share everything with you. I dream of you every night!*

Ramas stepped forward while Teo and Sunrise turned then walked down the beach. He reached around her bare waist and pulled her to him. *I have felt you inside me for long time, but you be too young. I wait and wait. No other girl make me feel that!*

After gazing into his wide eyes, Joanaa shared the first real kiss of her life. It told her all she needed to know. As they clung to each other, driven by ecstasy, her halo encompassed Ramas and together they floated above the sand.

Caught up in the moment, he did not even realize his feet weren't touching sand. Her warm kiss overtook him. Many deep breaths later, he looked down and, without words, snapped back to her gaze.

Yes, she assured him, *we're not held by gravity. I'm doing it but want you to join me! I show you, okay?*

On Fakarava, wedding celebrations still took place just as they had back before escaping, but commitments were private. *I yours, you mine!*

Yes. She added, "Ramas my love, I'm special, and I be sure you, too. I share all with you. I need to take you someplace, but, before we go, I want you to make love with me. I need to be joined to you."

Ramas tried to speak and could only force out the question, "Joined?"

We make love. Real love.

Without any further words, Joanaa wrapped her arms and her aura around the man she had loved since early womanhood. Floating up in a veil of white coral sand, dancing and spinning, the two virgins mated. Dolphins, generally uninhibited in their mating habits among their pod, gave them privacy and swam out to deep water. But the act was much too beautiful to ignore, so they stopped to watch from afar.

Time dilated and stretched. At last, Joanaa dropped the sand curtain and then set the breathless pair back upon the beach. Ramas's head was spinning.

My god, Joa, what just happened? Was that you? Was that us? Did it really happen?

She tried to explain. *Rama, it was me, but you, too. Your love made me more, made it happen. That's why I want you join me in a journey. You go with me?*

I with you for life. You go, I go.

Smiling, she sent sand swirling around them again. Their friends saw it from afar and returned. Joanaa and Ramas were ready for the journey. Blaze and Sur returned, as well, completing the wedding party. They knew this pledge. As it was with humans, it was with dolphins: when they chose, it was for life.

Four witnesses listened to the young lovers' vows. Just like Ramas, Joanaa forsook jargon. It was too informal for this moment. She linked, *Rama, I've been waiting so long.* Through her tears, she continued, *I will grow to my full womanhood with you by my side. I will stay with you and by you forever!*

As he squeezed her small hand, she felt him trebling as he linked, *Since you were thirteen, I have seen you and cannot explain, but knew you were the one even then. I know not how or why I knew it, but for you I waited. I will stay with you and by you forever!*

The marriage of two Generation Fives included their Bime cells. Not fully understanding but now bound together by love, at that instant Joanaa and Ramos sensed a destiny unimagined just moments before. Together, they were to do something unrealized. This sensation washed over them. Each Bime by itself could not be so potent, but together, they felt something powerful lay ahead. What they were to do remained cloaked but undeniably felt: they had a destiny and were to fulfil within The Plan. They linked to Teo and Sunrise and found that their Bimes also had this premonition but nothing more.

No more words were needed. The four witnesses, two lovers, and millions of Bime cells bathed in the moment. Some winks later, Joanna said, *Ramas, I love you so. Now you go with me now?*

Where?

It's not far. In fact, it's here.

A small wisp left the sandy veil, falling into his hand, while the remainder began to swirl around them until its helix reached the beach to form a fairy ring encircling the two lovers. Joanaa was caught in the moment: she saw it but didn't process it was not her who had done this!

Linking to Sunrise, she said, *We go to the music. Feel you want to go, too, but us only this time.*

Expecting no answer, she began to lead Ramas to the Truth. With her spirit soaring, Joanaa enjoyed how easy it was now, with her lover by her side.

Now unified with Ramas, their entity experienced a far more powerful connection to the truth than Joanaa alone could conjure. Deep within, she knew, even before taking her new mate there, that it was meant to be this way, that her premonition of love being the ultimate power was correct. With one vision, they marvelled at the micro-cosmos and the music. After a long stay, they returned from their wondrous honeymoon. As their feet touched down on the soft sand, Joanaa knew she would never be alone again.

Before letting go of their first meld, she paused. *My Ramas, I am now very sure that only one thing is more powerful than the music. Love cannot be manipulated. Its frequency is the same in every universe. It binds all together!*

Then the work began, as the four pioneers refined their knowledge and control, always with the goal that they would become skilled enough to tutor the entire Gen Five family. And when they had full control, they would be able to grant its use to their family in their greater quest to restore mankind on the Earth.

After many days' practice, the first four knew they were ready. Teo, Sunrise, Joanaa, and Ramas each took pairs of Bimes to the music. Upon returning, they demonstrated frequency control. Working in secret, each pair grew to their full potential and then, in turn, passed their skills forward until all mated pairs had been inducted.

They knew they must have a leader to represent them before the whole atoll family, when the time was right. By default, it was obvious that Joanaa was the one. Although she was the youngest, she would be the one to stand and speak before the family.

Her first wise act was to declare they must not leave their unmated Gen-5 brothers and sisters behind. Because she was the only single person to learn the truth, she knew they could achieve at least as much control as she herself had, before Ramas. They must not leave any Gen-Fives behind. They would be one in this quest to grant their powers to the whole atoll family. Then, when all was settled, they would use their power to restore mankind.

Next, Joanaa decided, as they explored and expanded their control, they could no longer meet there on that side of the lagoon. Using the craftiness inherited from Great-grandfather Artie, Joanaa devised transportation as unique as they were. It was nothing like anything ever seen in the world before.

Chapter 18

Full Awareness

AFTER CROSSING TO the far side of the rim, with Teo paddling their normal outrigger, the two lovers used their Bime epigenome and each infused two koa trees with Bios. It wasn't long before the trees began to morph and become the *Star Seeker* and *Far Away*.

These were ships far advanced from anything the world had ever seen. That is until now. Ships far advanced from any seen before: not so much built as given a mission, and they grew themselves into vehicles. For the moment, they resembled canoes, sleek and beautiful, but that shape was transitory. By design and link-directed re-growth, they went from normal trees into totally engineered canoes for now. With koa-Bios doing the work from within, they took shape cell by cell and became miracles. Although both of them were called canoes, in truth they were not.

Each one was thirty meters long and sprang from wood but became made of a composite material far superior to anything manmade. Not only were they strong but they arranged themselves for the best possible duty. True composites of fibers and resins bound them together, with each bio component duly engineered for strength.

There was a second and even more amazing bio-miracle: the canoe wood did not die when taken from its tree roots. It fed on the carbon exhalations of its passengers and their waste. Watered by warm tropical rain, their nutrition supplemented from sea minerals, it lived on and continued to host its bio-cells. The canoes were in symbiosis with their passengers, each depended upon the other. As much as the canoes carried the humans, the humans lovingly cared for the crafts.

Joanaa appointed bow leaders who formed links to their appointed steeds. It became a strong connection, human and canoe. After only two moon cycles to grow to maturity, the boats were launched.

Across the lagoon's rim, out of sight of the village, they paddled out for the first time, not because they had to do so but to be careful not to divulge any detail of the canoes' very different abilities. Nearly every action the Gen-Fives took was motivated by their concern that, once their superiority was revealed, the family might be repulsed or, worse, fear them and, worse still, reject them.

Finally, with practice at faking they were actually paddling the canoes, the Gen-Fives took the boats to the village side of the lagoon and carefully made it seem they could drag them above the waterline safely into the trees. With no fanfare, they let the family see them. Even studied carefully up close, the canoes looked like koa wood; in fact, the outer layer was koa. Soon, to the young people's relief, their journeys in the canoes were accepted as another aspect of the oddball Generation-Five kids.

Since their parents had no doubt they could take care of themselves, they were often allowed to disappear over the horizon, paddling and singing, not to return for days. Five years passed this way and they grew to their full potential, able to understand themselves and their immense power. Then they stopped aging and readied themselves for the revelation.

Joanaa's next edict was that the self-imposed restriction of not starting families would come to an end. If they were to reveal themselves to the family, the news that a new generation was coming might offset their rejection.

For the same human reasons Sunshine wished to bring forth Teo's baby, so Joanaa also wanted a child. It was time to take the truths to their Fakarava family with the hope it would not change their island music.

Chapter 19

New Leadership

JOEY LINKED TO THE family at Rory's request. Soon, they all gathered, sitting behind each of the twenty original escapees. Their downline spread out, fanlike, in what had become the gathering tradition. As usual, the fifth-generation youngsters weren't in their place at the back, but that was nothing new. The family almost expected odd behavior from them.

Rory spoke first. "Family, we have news! Our Bios tell us that our exile is over. I know you all understand what this means. We come together to discuss what we will do next. It is both joyous and ominous.

"Like you, I have come to love this place and do not want to fight a war. But, as Joey and I were reminded, this is about our rightful place on the Earth. We escaped here, to await this time, and now we must act. It is so.

"But I am uncomfortable planning our attack without the entire family. Does anyone here know how to reach them? And do you know where the Five-Gens go?" He scanned the gathering of his fellow Biomen and their Biom children. "Does anyone know?"

Fernando, the Nandy worker Joyce fell for before escaping on the last boat, stood up, indicating he wished to speak. Rory nodded, and he stepped forward. "Actually, I tried to find out once. I took Joyce out in our sailing canoe. With the sails up and adding our paddles, we can go as fast as anyone here. But there was no way we could keep up with those youngsters. I bet they went at least twice our speed. Either they must be really strong or we're getting old. I'm 125 and Joyce is 130!"

"You're not, Fernando," Rory chided him gently. "Remember, the Bios within maintain. You are stronger today than you ever were before Joyce kissed them into you! Now, go on."

"Okay, so, we even stood off once, to spot their direction. Then we followed. Still, when we got to where it looked like they were heading, on the other side of the atoll, where they would have landed, they were nowhere to be seen. For a time, we paddled up and down the lagoon's rim, thinking they might have turned, but still we found no kids and no canoes. Not even footprints in the sand. Like you, we couldn't link to them, either. But what really puzzles us is there's no pass-through to the open ocean anywhere near where they seemed to be going. It's over here on our side. Yet the canoe was nowhere to be seen!"

Joyce added, "If they went out of the lagoon, they'd need to drag their boats over the sand, but we didn't find a trace or track. It's almost like those things can fly! And another thing, there used to be giant koa trees over there, but they are gone now. We're pretty sure those kids made their giant canoes from them somehow, but I'll be darned if I could see how they could. Even Artie would have been challenged to drop them to the ground, let alone carve them! Have you seen the canoes, when they bring them to their meeting place up the beach? Big. Really big. And shaped so smooth and sleek?"

Lucy said, "They are our third grandchild's children's children. They are family. I'm sure there's a logical explanation for all these things. We'll just wait for them to return. But Rory, I think it's time for you and me to demand an explanation. No more trusting them. It's time to find out what they are up to!"

Ever practical, Artie added, "I'd also recommend, if the family feels we could proceed without them, that we at least begin to plan how we will return to take the world back. It seems to me we'll need every adult we can muster for the Return War! It's time to accelerate their development into mature adults. I know you parents have chosen to let them come into adulthood at the normal human rate and, of course, you get the final say, but the century-long exile is over." Pausing to let what he'd said sink in, he finished, "Our chances of survival, much less success, are nearly zero. But the odds *aren't zero!*" he nearly shouted. "We carry trillions of Bios allies and probably have the great advantage of surprise. We need an army, though, if we're to win the war!"

Grand-grandmother Lucy spoke next. "I am opposed and speak only for my great-grand, Joanaa, but I believe it is best for all our fifth-generation youngsters. Did we not decide to let them have a normal childhood here, or at least as close as possible? So, isn't that what they are doing—being independent, adventuresome, and learning about life? Too soon, all our lives will be pure hell. So, for now, let them be. We have all the generations present, from one to four, and since we're only missing the kids, how much can they contribute? I oppose aging them but agree with my husband on this. Let us begin planning our return without them."

Rory nodded his thanks to Joyce and Fernando, then spoke again, himself. "Thanks, Artie. Just like escaping from California, we need a basic framework of how we'll proceed. What's the first thing an invasion needs to do?"

Artie had already worked out that vital first step. "We need an advanced scouting sortie, to figure out what we're up against. We need to see what kind of creatures the Alphas have created to take our place. We need to know how many there are and how they might be defeated."

"He's right," Joey said, "but how can we get there undetected?"

Artie said, "Actually, I'm betting we won't need to go all the way back to the North Continent. We can go to the Hawaiian Islands. I'm pretty sure the communication satellites are still operational, because one of the goals, which seemed obvious when we left, was the Alphas were aiming at better links. But I'm also betting, after the genocide, the spy satellites had no purpose. We have evidence they aren't operational, since we've not been discovered here. It's a pretty good bet they let them decay and fall back to Earth. We won't be noticed crossing the ocean this time, no matter how we go. No hiding."

"That's fine, but, although the Islands are so much closer, how can we get there?" Lucy asked. "Is the New Horizon in any shape to make the voyage? One hundred years must have taken its toll on the old girl."

Artie explained, "Actually, I sunk her in the lagoon after we arrived, along with all the other boats that came after us. The last one brought Joyce and Fernando. Would any part of it be useful?"

"No," Artie explained, "like the others, it was a wood boat—slow and cheap to buy. Sorry, but I'm sure it's decayed into nothing by now."

Rory said, "I wasn't too sure the Triad or Uni didn't have satellites that might spot us back then. Before I did take the Mason drive out, thinking we'd need it here in the village. In fact, we've never used it or the scuba compressor, either. But to do so, we need to construct new boats. And now we're back to the kids. How the heck did they take down the koa trees? And what did they do with the wood? They could have made pretty good boats."

"I seriously doubt the salvaged rigging on any of the derelicts will take sailing," Artie said, "but the Mason drive can power us to Hawaii and back. Once we've built it, I can reinstall it as an auxiliary engine."

"Tomorrow," Rory instructed, "let's dive on all the sunken boats. Each one got us here safely. There's a slim chance we might rebuild one to do the scouting mission. Then, when we know what we face, we can plan how we'll get back to the North. So we have step one—a boat to Hawaii, to scout them. And then return here for part two, which will involve building bigger and more transport boats to take us to the war.

"We can store up food and water and maybe entice a couple of Joanaa's trained dolphins to go with us, to catch fish to eat. I'm sure you've seen, she's done wonders with them."

Joyce added, "Now that you mention it, we've noticed how they stay around their canoes when they paddle. It looks like she's trained an entire pod!"

Rory took the lead back. "Right, Artie. I'm so glad we have you to handle these mechanical things. We'd be lost without you! Now, what else can we do?"

"Not much until we know what we're facing," Artie replied. "For now, let's get a hull back floating. I call on my entire downline of children to help. Please divide yourself into two teams. From the games, we know which of us are strong. They should be on my team, to bring up whatever hull we choose. The others will start gathering supplies."

"Okay, Artie, you get started," Rory confirmed. "That will take several days. By then, the kids should be back, and we can tell them about the reason we're sending the sailboat out. For now, let's withhold telling them about the accelerating maturity until we're sure the invasion is going to happen.

Chapter 20

New Revelations

FOUR DAYS LATER, the canoes came gliding over the horizon. But this time, they came directly to the village, not to their landing place up the rim. Unknown to the clan, the Fives had finished their final retreat. They, too, had made some big decisions.

Universally, they had agreed it was time to take their rightful place in the clan and show the family their unique powers. After five years' work on their skills, the Fives were ready to reveal themselves for what they were: powerful, very powerful. And yet they were also still fearful of rejection by their loved ones. Joanaa was to be their spokesperson, although they could all link as one entity now. They just didn't think the clan could accept the power of that, at first.

Joanaa would begin by explaining how she had discovered the music and then introduced the others to it, starting with small surprises. The canoes would be another good place to begin.

As they paddled in close to the beach, the bow leader linked, *Look! They come to greet us!*

Rory and Joey, along with several other clan people, came down to the water's edge and started to wade in.

The Fives' canoes were an impressive thirty meters long, so the elders expected the youngsters would need help skidding them up under the trees. Rory himself stepped into waist-deep water and placed his hand on the gunnel, remarking, "Wow!

These canoes are amazing! Did you make them from the trees across the lagoon? I'm sure Artie will want to hear all about how you built them."

Joanna stood up from her command seat, stepped out of the boat, and approached Rory. She spoke with no jargon, as that was rarely used since the Gen-Fives unified their persona. "Great-grandfather, your timing couldn't be better. We made a big decision today. It's time to tell you many things. With your permission, we wish to do this from the circle, before the whole family. I speak for us. I am their leader.

"But first," she said, "let me answer your question. We did not make the canoes in the normal way. We introduced Bios into them while the trees were still standing. The trees then began to form our canoes. Letting them use their own epigenome to modify themselves, they knew they were sturdy but not strong enough for the task ahead. So, they set out to change their own structure. Their fibers are set for maximum strength now, not like normal wood. The resin is also organic but stronger than anything manmade."

Turning to Artie, who had a deep knowledge of mechanics and engineering, Joanaa added, "You see, Great-grandfather, all composite materials are fibers and resins. So is normal wood— cellulose and resin. Our canoes are also fiber, but it has the properties of a spider web, stronger than carbon. The resin is organic and it's also totally superior. Our composites are stronger than anything manmade yet. They are bio-made!"

Surprise number one was on the table. Rory turned to Artie and asked, "You ever hear of anything like that?"

"No. Never," he replied. "So, you are using our virus partners to modify the world around you?"

At this point, Ramas stepped up beside Joanna, and they joined hands. Knowing this next revelation was going to be difficult, she held her chin high. "Great-grandmother Lucy, my grandparents…" She looked until she spotted her birth mother. "Mother, Father, you must know Ramas and I are joined."

Puzzled and disappointed, Ramas's mother, Suron, asked, "Why didn't you come to the village and let us join you in the way? Why did you not let us share the joy?"

Ramas said to his mother, "Momma, please forgive us, but we had to do it this way. I am so sorry for keeping it a secret. We've been paired for five years. I love you and Papa with all my heart, but I'm in love with Joanaa. Please be happy for us! I'm so sorry for revealing this in this way, but hear us out, and maybe you can forgive us. Each one of is paired—it was necessary to be able to control the music."

With furrowed brow, Rory asked, "The music? What's that? And another question—what do you mean 'the trees knew'?"

Joanaa linked privately, *Going too fast, lover! Too much.* Ramas nodded; he understood.

Knowing that her small announcement was nothing compared to what was ahead, Joanaa said, "I promise, Grandfather, we will reveal all when we assemble the family. We have decided it is time to let you know the whole truth. But we all want you to know that nothing we've done or will tell you has any motive other than love and respect for our wonderful family."

To reassure Rory and the elders, Joanaa turned to the two boats. Each bow leader nodded. "Yes, we grew the canoes. But that's such a small part of what we have to tell you. Before we answer any more of your questions, we ask Grandmother Joey to call the clan to the meeting circle. We've had many meetings by ourselves, but our last secret meeting has now finished. Today, it's time to grant our powers to the family."

"*Powers?*" Rory almost choked on his response.

By prior agreement, the Gen-Fives withheld their Bime links and the amazement they had in store for their family.

Even so, Rory felt Joanaa's energy and resolve. Wordlessly, he linked to Joey, *Go ahead call the family back. Something big is going on with our Fives.*

As he did this, to the crowd's shock and amazement both canoes rose above the water with their crews still seated inside. Then, Joanaa wheeled around, gestured up the beach, and walked ahead. Silently, the boats flanked her, gliding beyond the tide line within the shade of the coconut trees, where they settled down gently.

Joanaa turned to Rory, the family's former leader, held out her hand, and said, "As you can see, we have much to discuss! *Much*," she repeated.

In short order, the whole family came to the meeting circle. Each sat in order, a concentric circle of the Biomen pioneers with Joey and Rory standing in the middle with space to pace. Everyone fully expected the Gen-Fives to sit in their assigned order but were not totally surprised when they didn't, just remained standing at the back.

At last, Joanaa squeezed through and stood next to Rory.

He stood formally and said, "We meet to discuss our plans to return to our rightful place on the Earth. This is an entire family mission, as you know." He held back any reminder of their forming the scouting mission. "But before we begin, at this time I wish all in the circles to join with me in my link." Then he added, *Joanaa has requested to speak. I grant it.*

Beyond Rory's understanding and to his disapproval, the twenty Gen-Fives withheld their link. He wondered whether this was an act of rebellion What did they have to hide? But he had granted Joanaa the floor and was resolved to let her say her message before chastising them. After all, they were just kids, he reasoned. It probably was a bigger deal to them than it would be for the adults.

Joanaa also stood, as a leader. Turning to Rory and Joey, she then swept her hand around the inner circle and spoke aloud, without links. "Great-grandfathers and grandmothers, uncles and cousins, we come here today to do something we've anticipated with great joy, but also with great concern that you'll not accept our gift. We assure you we do it out of love and respect.

"For five years, we have worried about this day, for it means our family will change forever. Our mission remains the same— to put mankind and all their bio-partners in their rightful place.

"But we are fearful because it will challenge the very foundation of our clan." With that, she motioned to Ramas, who walked forward through the seated crowd and took his place by her side. "This is my life's mate. I am pregnant by him."

The family sighed, especially Artie and Lucy. The great-grandparents were relieved at this big announcement, that a Gen Six on the way. *Great!* they linked, and the others joined in the congratulations.

Rory linked to Joey, *You see, it's important but not earth-shaking! She's old enough to have children now. By my reckoning, she's twenty-three.*

He started to step in front of her to resume control of the meeting, but she swept her hand over the eighteen Fives still beyond the circle. She linked to them, *Remain on the ground and walk as humans. We are here not to amaze, but to join.*

They spread out to their family branch then, touching shoulders as they snaked through the circles, they came to the front and stood.

Joanaa motioned for the circles to move back and waited. Although this simply looked like people scooting on sand, it was far more than that. It was the end for the Biomen's rule. Joanaa's heart hurt, but she knew it had to be done. She also knew the family wouldn't just rearrange, at first. This was *against* the way of the family. She turned to Ramas and asked, "Is it time?"

He linked back, *Yes, I think so.*

She turned to address Rory. "I'm so sorry, Grandfather. But when you hear us out, you'll understand. You see, Grandma Lucy was right. It *is* a matter of our energy but not like what you imagine. First, we know much of the truth of the universe. But more, we control much of it. We have also learned to control time. Time is part of the continuum, and it has a frequency in each universe. We can adjust ours up or down."

She gestured to her mate. "A demonstration. Ramas, walk over to the far side of the circle." The families parted to let him pass. "Now, do not close his path back. Ramas, return to me as we discussed."

Instantly, her mate flashed from his position outside the circle to her side. To those watching, it seemed as though he was teleported. In truth, all he did was walk at a normal pace, but within his skewed time.

All the family members gasped!

"You see," Joanaa continue, "Ramas squeezed his time within his influence. But he kept his sphere close in to him, so it didn't affect yours. He did so by adjusting his frequency. We Fives can all do this and much more!"

Rory forced himself to speak. "I have many questions. How did you discover this? And can you grant it to us?

"I am sorry," she replied. "We cannot, but we can join in the fight using it."

Ramas said, "If it wasn't for Joanaa and her explorations, we might never have uncovered our uniqueness. That is part of the reason we have chosen her as our leader."

Rory asked, "I must ask again do you think that Generation-Fives are now clan leaders?"

"We do," Ramas said, "but not by a rebellion. That would be wrong. You have now seen but two of our powers, with others yet to be revealed. Do you not agree we have grown beyond the four generations before us? We are a newly evolved species, yet we are still your children and family members. Can you accept that we, led by Joanaa, should be at the front of the circle?"

An awkward silence befell the family. As they all exchanged glances, nods, and small talk, the Gen-Fives waited. They always knew this was not going to be easy. Finally, the standoff ended as, one by one, each family slid back, as a group. The standing Fives settled down into their new seats at the front of the circle.

Rory could hold off no longer. "Okay, Joanaa, I understand you feel your powers make you our leader. But what about wisdom? You haven't lived enough life to have much of it—or do you *think* you do? Do you recall the story of the Uni Regents who took over world dominion by default? They, too, were very smart, but they also lacked wisdom. Their leadership proved to be a disaster!"

"I know, Grandpa. Please understand, we're here in complete respect. It's just that..." Breathing deeply, she hesitated before beginning again. "It's that we are different from you." She withheld saying "superior."

From the second row, Lucy spoke up. "Of course you are different, honey! We're so proud of you—tall, strong, and so beautiful. You're full of energy, and we love to see it. But why do these powers make you our leaders?"

Okay, every Bime, it's time, Joanaa linked. *Open your links, but do it very slowly. They are much more fragile than you. When the time is right, I'll let you find your family links and start toward full understanding, each family learning from you.*

At her command, each of the Bimes let their mind-to-mind links open just enough for the family to feel their immensity, compared to their own. The family members all fell silent in wonder. They could feel but not grasp how powerful the Five minds had become.

Joanaa spoke with words for the last time. "Can you sense how much more powerful your children's minds are than yours? I must tell you they have only let you peek into them! If we linked with our entire Bime minds, it would overpower you. We restrain ourselves for your sake. From now on, I will speak in my link to you all."

She began, *We are more than bio-human combinations, as you all are, to one degree or another. Yes, our parents were as close to Bime as any generation could be. But only we are truly a new species.* She quickly added, *Still, we are as human as any of you. We love, we fear, and we hope.*

The evolution happened when we were in our mothers' wombs. Our parents' Bios had evolved, too, at what seemed to be a preordained time. An epigenome file, unseen until our gestation, opened. Seeing the potential of it, but remembering their first promise, the Bios asked us if we would allow the change. It seemed like our destiny, so we each linked agreement. You see, Gen-Fives had their Bime minds formed during gestation.

After allowing time to let the family process, she went on. *The new file created new structure. Every cell in our bodies is not a symbiosis of Bios and human, as you are. It is a combination. We're not partners with Bios. We are human Bios. We're Bime! Bime!* she emphasized.

We are the next phase in what has become clear, THE Plan. We have not forgotten what it is to be human, but we are much more. With no grandeur intended, just her love for her family, she wept. *We hope— No, we truly pray you will accept us as we are! If you cannot, we will leave, but with all our hearts we don't want to do so. This island is our home and you are our family.*

Rory again linked, *So now, my time as clan leader is over. I must say it's without regret, as it's been a burden for the hundred years. But I do have reservations. It's time to retire or at least take a different role in the family, along with Joey, Artie, Lucy, and the rest.*

But I am not willing to do that until I come to have faith in your wisdom. Your superior makeup and powers are becoming clear to me, but I also believe you cannot be a good leader without wisdom. Life teaches us patience, introspection, and so many more lessons. For now, we must discuss how we will proceed.

After taking time to process Rory's edict, Joanaa began again. *I will link one more thing then we will go away to let you discuss this without fear of hurting our feelings. We dearly love you. We have many powers yet to reveal, and we can help achieve the mission. We're not here to take over except by your wishes and consent. But the true question is can you accept we are superior to you?*

That last sentence stung to the core. For one hundred years, the people of the village had believed themselves fully capable of retaking the Earth, but truly they had had no idea how. Long before the Reyton revolution, several scientists and star-gazers had warned of first contact probably not going well. Alien visitors would surely be superior and possibly not friendly, they'd predicted.

While their Gen-Four parents saw them as their children, the whole family tried not to see them as aliens invading their world. Still, the thought was there. The Gen-Fives were loved and admired, but could they be trusted? Would they always use these unrevealed powers for good? An then there was an inescapable question: did they have an agenda of their own?

Joanna linked, *Rise, please my Bime sisters and brothers. Meet me at the canoes, and close your links to your precious families. We will leave for a time. Hopefully, we will be welcomed back soon. For now, they have much to discuss without us! Rise now."*

Silently, twenty forms unlinked with the clan and then rose up off the sand, gliding quietly out of the circle. It seemed to those left behind that their friendly lagoon music had suddenly changed.

Chapter 21

Acceptance through Love

RORY FELT STUNNED TO HIS core as he resumed his spot in the family circle's center. No longer making a speech, he didn't stand nearly as tall when he asked, "What do we do now? Artie, you're always the one who grounds us. What are you thinking?"

"I... well, *uh,* I actually don't know. I just watched my great-great-granddaughter float out the door, heading to god knows where," Artie replied. "I'm sorry, Rory, but me and my Bios are... we're... Well, I guess we're... Geez! I don't even have the words. Bios, you got any?"

We've always sensed we weren't using the entire epigenome, not unlike your partial use of your former human brains. But nothing came of it. It would seem that these young ones have unlocked it. Other than that, we offer no wisdom.

Rory asked again, "There are eighteen original Biomen and one hundred eighty Biom offspring here. Surely somebody has a clear thought, no?"

Stunned at the new development, there was not one comment from the family until Artie broke the silence. "Rory, I ask for you to stop the gathering and let us think. I need time alone with Lucy and our family branch. Can we please come back tomorrow?"

"Yes, of course," Rory replied. "Go, collect your thoughts. We'll all do the same. After one hundred and one years, another day won't make a lot of difference."

Campfires burned nearly through the night as families gathered. They all seemed to be clinging to their beliefs. Knowing that the next day was going to be monumental, they had to make a choice.

Dawn broke on a somber village. Many family members had not slept. Rory asked Joey to call them all together, and once they were seated in their usual circles, he linked his thoughts. *I have a few questions that can't be answered. First, we're amazed that their Bime links never touched our Bios! They can close us out. Can we do that to them? How did they keep it from us for all these years—almost since they were born, or even before? And where do they go when they're not here?*

He continued, *Here's one that may be within our ability… Gen-Fours, do you now recall the change made to your reproductive systems? Is it still there? Can you have more children?*

Parents and their Bios answered, *We see it now, and we're amazed we didn't see it sooner.*

Surrat linked, *Rory, are you suggesting we have more children, if they do leave us? I speak for myself and their father, since we are Joanaa's parents. They are our children, and if they leave, we go with them! They may be demi-gods, but I don't need anything beyond my mother's heart to know they need our love and, more, they need our wisdom to control their power.*

Others in the circle linked, *We agree. They are our family, our children.*

Grandparents, aunts, and uncles chorused in unison, *They are ours. We are theirs! We stay together!"*

No further discussion was necessary; the decision was made. They had to trust their offspring and relinquish leadership to the youngsters, whose full powers had yet to be revealed.

But Rory, having lived in the early times, voiced a real concern. *Here's the thing I'm sure I share with those of us who lived in the Uni times. This could become a repeat of the Regents. While it was the Alphas we ran from, they, too, would have stopped us if they knew about our Bios.*

Joey joined her husband, linking, *Although they played a small role, they were part of the reason we came here. Those misguided Regents—or should I say* unguided *Regents—also began as sincere young people. These youngsters seem sincere and loving. Given that they honed their abilities for five years before coming forth to reveal them, obviously they can control their power. I agree with all of you. We stay together as a family. But the second matter is what I'm worried about—leadership!*

Surrat stood and spoke. *I have an answer for that. You are right, the Regents were unguided, but our children are not. They have a solid set of four generations to guide them.*

Artie added, *She's right. Having too much power consumed the Regents. But there's even more to support what Surry says The Regents had no real purpose, but we do. We are committed to retake the world from the Alphas. The Gen-Fives have guidance and purpose. I say let's let them take over, but with the eighteen pioneers remaining as counsellors, and with voting rights, too.*

Lucy spoke again. *That didn't take long. We remain one family with a deeper, more capable leadership. But now what? How do we tell them they are welcome?*

Rory suggested, *I suspect they can hear our links even though we don't sense it. They are our children and perhaps the best hope humanity has.*

With nothing to herald their appearance, neither sound nor light, the Fives appeared just then in the inner circle.

Slack-jawed, Artie gulped. "Okay, that was just freaky! Were you here all the time? Invisible? Oh, is that part of your mystery powers? Do I want to know?"

Through flowing tears, with unlinked words, Joanna spoke. "We weren't here or invisible. Someday, we'll tell you where we were. But for now, let it be known we were not eavesdropping on you, either. We respect your wisdom, and we welcome it. The real truth is we felt your hearts and your love. They pulled us here.

"There is a power that dwarfs our power, and we all have it. You, too. We Fives sense, without knowing, that there is a Plan and it is driven by love. We don't understand it, yet we know in the center of our being that the power of love is *THE* foundation.

Switching to linking, she added, *Thank you for accepting us as we are. We promise we will never abuse our power and will always seek your council. Now I say to my command, go to your parents and their family!*

Each of the Fives raced to their mother and father with open arms. They clung to one another with great relief, the burning question answered: the family had accepted them.

Rory noted the joy around him, but also he understood the pain on Joanaa's face as she watched. He took her by the hand while gesturing to her mother and father and family to follow them to the circle center. *You see my great-great-granddaughter, already you are learning how leadership weighs. Your duty kept you centered, didn't it? No worries. We'll come to you. One more giant hug for the new leader.*

Entwined, Joanaa choked back tears as she declared, *I am the new leader of this clan, and we will not be denied our destiny. I accept that I need wisdom and I promise to counsel with Rory, Joey, and all the other originals. Through them, each family may—* She stopped herself. "Will" *advise and counsel me.*

She waited for what seemed too short of a time, given how they had worried about this moment for five years. Once it ended, the families sat and turned their attention to their new commander. *We can plan our war another day. Today, we celebrate like we've never done before. We'll sing and dance and swim with our dolphin generations!*

Chapter 22

A New Destiny, A New Path

WE HAVE MUCH TO reveal about them, too, Joanna continued to the assembled families. *Our dolphin friends are not trained. They live freely as bio-partners. After we gained their trust, these Bios-enhanced friends revealed to us they have always had equal intelligence to humans, but they wisely chose to live without technology or reveal themselves fully to us.*

Just look at the carefree life they've lived for all their generations! They mate for life, have loving children, play in the ocean, and never go to war. They do not worry or stress about anything. They each have a family leader, which can be a male or female. If full truth is known, their lives were always far superior to our former ones back in our over-developed world. We believe they, too, are part of the Plan. Now that they are imbued with Bios, as the elders are, you can link to them as easily as to us. Biofins, I grant that you may link to the whole family.

Pausing to emphasize the next pronouncement, she added, *I have another reason to celebrate. Every single female in this generation is now pregnant! Now, that's something to celebrate, isn't it? Soon, we'll have a family of Gen-Sixers!* After a round of gleeful cheering, she pronounced, *Tomorrow, we plan our invasion and destiny. Today, we celebrate our love!*

The sun rose with only a few Biomen, Biom, and only two Bimes in the meeting circle. Hungover not from the free-flowing kava, they were all still overwhelmed with emotion. Long after sunrise, the remaining family members wandered into the circle. As another leadership lesson, Joanna and Ramas had restrained from partaking, so they were there to greet the clans as they came in.

Good morning, family. Sit as you would. From now on, we are all one. You should sit with your family, but in no particular order. Everyone has an equal say. Now, we begin to plan. She raised her arms in a defiant gesture, shouting, "We will retake our Earth!"

Artie once again offered the leadership his commonsense warning. "Hold on, Joanaa. We have no idea what we'll find back in the alpha world. We must send scouts to see what we'll be facing when we invade. It's been one hundred years. A few more days won't mater. I've been raising the New Horizon, and it's almost ready for the voyage. But now I can see that your canoes are how we'll go."

Ramas stepped forward. "Artie, we appreciate what you say, and we link agreement. Truly, we need not go in the ancient sailboat. I'm sorry you've spent the effort getting it ready for the journey. I know you are attached to it, as all sailors are, but we have a far better way!"

"I know I speak for all," Artie continued. "Isn't it time to tell us what the hell they are?

"Like all of us Bimes," Ramas explained, "our canoes are far different from yours. True, they are vehicles and can travel."

"So what?" Artie challenged. "The New Horizon can travel, too. It got us here, didn't it? And it safely delivered the second wave, too!"

Yes, Artie, Ramas replied, switching to linking. *It did. But hear me out. When we say travel, we don't mean in the usual sense. We mean it can transcend distances. I hate to play the teacher with one of my idols, but what's the basic formula for velocity?*

Artie had no problem linking that answer. *Velocity equals distance divided by time.*

Right, but you've already seen we can compress time. We've truly enjoyed Fernando and Joyce trying to track us, as we left the rim. Fernando, did you ever come close?

Not even, he answered, adding, *I always suspected those canoes weren't normal.*

They aren't, I assure you. We have no idea how quickly they can transport us. We're still learning about that. Not only were they custom-grown by Bios, but they can time travel. Okay, let me restate that we can compress our time when we travel, and our canoes go with us. Unlike all our space-farers before us, we no longer expend energy trying to go faster. We just change the frequency of time and go much quicker! Understand?

"So, you can compress time to encompass your canoes, too?" Artie asked. "Can you then go faster than light?"

We're not sure. But if we can, the stars aren't far away. We might travel the universe.

So, we don't change time. We compress our relationship to time. Time is relative and depends on the frequency of the universe. Our time accelerates by adjusting our universal frequency out of phase with your time. Take Ramas's demonstration the other day. The walk he would have made in your time would have taken maybe five winks. But he accelerated his time to far less than yours, so he could cross in less than a fraction of a wink relative to your time. Understand?

I think I get the concept, Artie replied, *but how?*

Artie, I don't want to hurt your feelings, but for you to understand, we'd need to show you the universal truth. It has to do with the frequency of the entire universe and the final basic building blocks of pure energy. All things are made of them, including us. We de-synchronize ourselves relative to elements and entities around us.

Artie sounded curious and eager. *I sort of understand what you are saying, so now I'm ready show me how to do it!*

Pausing, for he knew it would sting, Ramas demurred. *Sorry, you cannot go where we went to discover these things. Without that knowledge, I cannot explain to you how it is done. You, along with all generations before us, are not capable! But even if you were, it took us five years' practicing to learn to fully control our abilities. So, if you accept us, then we offer our use of these powers to win the war.*

Rory put his arm around Lucy and then spoke. "So, that's what you were doing on those excursions you were always taking? Gaining strength and control of your abilities?"

"It is."

Beginning to see that the discussion was heading toward too much tech and knowing they had more pressing matters, Joanaa stepped in. "Thank you, Grandfather Rory, Artie, and Ramas!

"Family, for my first battle command, I order one canoe go to the mainland, *not* Hawaii, and discover what we face, if we attack. Wait. I correct myself. *When* we attack! We must know what the new server animals are like. Can we defeat the Alpha world? What will be our Bios and Bime losses?"

"Bime losses?" asked Joey.

"Yes. You see, were not bios and human cells as you are, we are one, and when the Alphas discover that, they will try to kill us entirely. Your Bios within will suffer great losses, and you will endure the pain but survive. We might not!"

Turning to the canoe crew, she said, "You are to leave immediately! Star Seeker. With my male crew members only, not the females. Pregnant wives and the second canoe will remain behind. Because the bow leader of my canoe is a woman, I will be the only woman to go in her place."

Rory leapt up at this. "No, Joanaa! This is the wisdom we elders can contribute. I know you want to go. I would, too. In fact, I'd go now, if you commanded it."

"Sorry, Grandfather, but you would be in too much danger, something we can avoid."

"Are you saying I couldn't accelerate when your crew compresses their time? If they do it and the canoe is encompassed within their synchronous sphere, why couldn't I be encompassed, too?"

Joanna linked back, *We believe we could bring you along, but we're not sure. The only way to find out would be to try it, and we are not willing to risk losing any one of you to find out.*

The canoes are also alive, you see. When we harvested them, they did not die. They are self-healing. But we've never tried to enfold any generation other than ours. But that's not my greatest worry. We can literally disappear, if we're detected or threatened back in Alpha society. You cannot. And unless you were within our sphere at the time, we might need to leave you behind. You see, we have much more practice and training to do, if we're to use generations before ours in the war.

Okay, Rory linked in response. *I understand I cannot go. But neither can you. I only wanted you to understand that, as a leader, you often make choices you don't like. I truly feel your anguish at staying behind. Besides, what about your unborn child? You wouldn't want to risk it, would you? If you are lost, we not only lose you but the future-gen, too! If you are so superior to us, what might your child be?*

Joanna shook her head as she processed this warning and then looked up to meet his eyes. Without turning away from his stern gaze, she said with pain in her voice, "My crew will go without me. You are right. I realize. Bovie, go with Far Away's bow leader. Go now without me! Compress your time and be safe.

"Since distance means nothing, go to San Francisco Bay, not Hawaii. Observe and report back when you have a sense of what we face in the upcoming war." Pointing toward the northwest horizon, Joanna added, "Bime speed and be safe, my family! We stay linked by love."

Gesturing his crew to him, Bovie rose, then he and nine scouts on the amazing Bio-Koa canoes flashed out.

Silence enveloped the circle. Lucy stood and articulated a simple wish. "May my great-great-granddaughter's command come to be!"

Days passed on Fakarava. The families worried. Like many generations of seafarers' wives, they waited, looking out to the vast water.

On the fourth day after the scouts' departure, the sun rose. From habit, Rory rolled over to enfold Joey, but his hand fell on the empty mat. Sitting up, he saw her silhouette as the dawn shone through her sarong. Facing away from him, she was staring out to the horizon.

He rose, walked to her side, and put his arms around her. "I'm worried, too. I know those kids are powerful, but do they have the self-control to not do something stupid? I know they control their power, but are they in control of their *emotions*? What if—?"

She spun around and put her hand on his lips. "I won't hear it. They will be okay!"

"I hope you're right," Rory said. "I wish I could pray. It's just they should have been back days ago. How much time does it take to observe what the Earth is like by now? Joanaa hasn't heard any link from them since three days ago, either, and if you remember, she gave them no specific length of time to be gone. Or did she? Maybe she linked it to them?"

"I have no idea. But those kids are pretty resourceful. Keep in mind, they can flash out, if need be."

"I know," he said, "but I also know they won't do that, if it might tip the Alphas and their new servers to the fact that they have failed to eliminate all human life from the planet. They cannot be discovered or we will lose the element of surprise, which I suspect will be crucial, if we are to exterminate the Alphas and their server animals."

Finding nothing reassuring to say further, he pulled Joey close enough to feel the comfort of her breasts. He feared the worst. They stared together at the sunrise and hoped.

Eventually, he broke the silence. "Put on your pandanas. Let's go to the circle and wait for them. We ought to be seen there when the others come. Link to Joanaa to meet us there."

Joey pulled away, flung her sarong over her shoulder, and they walked slowly toward the clearing. As they entered, they were rewarded to find others arriving.

Rory waited to see if Joanaa would speak. He was feeling like he should say something reassuring, but he wanted her to be the one to do it. She looked at him and then slowly shook her head. Reading it without a link, he stepped to the speaker's platform. Joey put her arm around Joanaa and hoped her man, wizened by one hundred, forty-five years of life, could find the words to lift the mood.

Joanaa was at a loss as to what she could say to the clan. "Grand-grandfather, you've been through so much heartache in your life. How do we deal with losing ten of our loved ones?"

It didn't take their newly realized Bime links to feel her anguish. Rory carefully chose each word. "Family, I know these children. They are smart and they are—"

A whoosh of sand flew all around them just then, as the Star Gazer swooped up the beach and stopped quite close to the outer circle. Red-faced, Bonvie stepped over the side, while his crew remained in the canoe.

"Joanaa, Grandfather, my family, I apologize for the poor entrance. It's just that we have some important and unexpected news." Regaining a bit of composure, he spoke as an officer. "Joanaa, Grand-grandfather, Grand-grandmother Joey, Lucy, Artie, and all the generations to follow, we spent days observing life as it has changed, and we must report that—"

Rory held up his hand. "Joa, with your permission, I believe the news can wait. It's been one hundred and five years since we escaped the Alphas. A few more hours can't hurt. For now, find your wives and family. Welcome home! You have no idea how worried we were. We are so glad to see you are safe! Now please, go to your loved ones."

He turned to Joanaa and winked. "I mean if that is okay with Joanaa. Can't the news wait until the welcome homes are finished?"

To laughing and cheers, all nine scouts leaped over the gunnels to hug their wives. Bonvie remained in the bow but locked loving eyes upon his mate, hoping she would understand that duty came first. He then announced, "I will wait to offer the news to the elders. It's my duty."

Joanaa stepped up close beside her grand-grandfather; she was beginning to see why the family leadership must be shared, for he had qualities she was yet to gain. She nudged against him to say she understood his wisdom. Holding tight to Ramas's hand, she said, "Yes, Commander Bonvie, it is your duty, but not now. I command you go to your wife. All scouts, you need time with your family. We will reconvene this afternoon. Go now."

Rory looked down at Lucy and Artie's greatest granddaughter, winked one more time, and said nothing. Ramas led Joanaa away not slowly.

Chapter 23

Mission or Missionaries?

SEVERAL HOURS PASSED. Joanaa linked to them all to re-join the circle. Once they reconvened, the low sun told them they hadn't a lot of day left.

"We will now learn what our scouts discovered, and then continue planning." She waved toward Bonvie and linked him to come forward. To all the Gen-Fives, she linked, *Remember how delicate their links are compared to ours. Slowly open only the portion that will enable all to see and hear your individual reports, please.*

As Bonvie began his report, images and sounds of the streets of San Francisco projected within each generation's mind, and above the circle, too. Other scouts shared their visions of the South Bay, where the original Reyton project once incubated new technologies. In turn, each of the Five crew members described what they had seen on their mission, being careful to not offer opinions.

Scene after scene floated in the air before the gathering, while the family watched in silence. They were amazed to see humans walking the streets, eating meals, and playing with what the island dwellers assumed were their children.

Life looked normal. Perhaps there were fewer people around, but not anywhere close to the degree they'd expected.

Joanaa turned to the pioneers and asked, "I do not know what normal life looks like back there, other than what you have told me in stories. But this seems quite normal to me. Is it?"

Several of the elders offered their observations, noting the cities appeared to be less populated but, otherwise, the people looked a lot like before they all fled. Artie noted it seemed less busy, less noisy. People looked less stressed; there was no apparent hustle and bustle. But, he had to admit, yes, while it was totally unexpected, everything seemed close to normal. The servers were human, and life continued as it had before they'd fled.

Then Joanaa proclaimed, "It would seem we must rethink our plan. The Alphas must have had a change of heart. Humans walk the Earth. Perhaps we have failed? Have we exiled ourselves for no reason?"

Rory jumped up to disagree. "No fucking way!" then he blushed, suddenly aware of his position. Generally, he tried never to show this kind of emotion, but it could be justified at the moment, given that the whole hundred years he had put them through, including all the sacrifice and hiding, now appeared to be for nothing. All that had happened during their century in exile was credited to his leadership and planning. None of it could be attributed to the others; it was all on him.

With his heart hammering, he stammered, "I... I'm... I'm the one who brought us here! It was all my idea, and it seems it was for nothing!"

Silence fell over the group. One by one, they walked away from the circle. Although everyone was relieved that their scouts had come back safely, each member of the family struggled with a very mixed set of emotions. The reporting did mean they could remain there, on Fakarava. It also confirmed they could move about the Pacific, if they wished. Their exile was over. But the news also told them they had removed themselves from society for no good reason and the thing that drove them, their return, was false.

Dark, depressing days followed. Their island music stopped. There was no village intercourse, no gatherings. No games or beach fires. Finally, motivated mostly by boredom, Artie asked to have the images transferred to his Bios-assisted brain. Joanaa requested the scouts to oblige him.

Using his mechanic's troubleshooting skills, Artie reviewed each picture over and over again. For reasons he couldn't explain, something bothered him about what he was seeing. Repeatedly, he studied and analyzed the smaller details. Finally, he leaped up and linked to Rory, Joey, Lucy, and Joanaa, *Come to the circle now. Right now! You, too, Joanaa and Ramas. Let the others wait. First, you should confirm what I've discovered with your own eyes.*

They came running and asked breathlessly, "What, Artie?"

He began his analysis. "Look at the people's feet!"

"Their feet?" Rory asked.

"Yes. Everyone, look again."

After several repeats, the three other elders finally saw what Artie has seen. Not Ramas or Joanaa, though, since they had no experience with normal behavior.

"Hey!" Lucy exclaimed, "they aren't stepping. They are kind of shuffling. Like, *uh*, well, like zombies!"

"That's right," Artie confirmed. "Now look at the families. What do you see?"

"Well," continued Lucy, "I see a man and a woman and a child. Nothing unusual."

"Don't you think it's strange that they are always a perfect, three-person set?" Artie asked. "One child, never two or three. Always walking, just walking, as though they are training or marching the child."

"You're right!" Rory said. "The Alphas must have instituted population control and taken away free will!"

Artie explained to Joanaa, "It took me a lot of time to see things. We four had forgotten what everyday life looked like, ourselves. First of all, we didn't have much of a normal life. We were so caught up in Reyton that we had removed ourselves from society. Then, given we've been here for a hundred years, it all looked normal, at first. But then, a couple of telling details finally dawned on me. See if you agree. It's definitely not normal life!

"Do you see any older people?" he continued. "Any grandparents in any of the scenes? Or do you see any mixed-race parents? And the biggest observation I made, what else do you see? Or maybe I should say what do you *not* see?"

After several repeat viewings, Lucy exclaimed, "Oh my God, they don't talk to each other, and they don't smile or laugh!"

Artie nodded. "You're right. Those people, if they truly are people—perhaps they just look like humans—are exhibiting programmed behavior."

Joanaa asked her grandparents, "Are you saying their behavior is far from what you would have done, had you remained there?"

"That's hard to answer, Joanaa," Lucy replied. "It certainly isn't what I would have expected to see. It seems like de-evolution or some kind of Alpha control. When we left, we were certain that the new Alpha servers would be far less inventive, more subservient."

"And physically smaller, more able to manipulate small items," added Artie. He continued, "From what I've seen, they are not free-willed people! The lazy Alphas have not killed the humans. It would have been a lot of epigenome work to make something new yet again. They just dumbed them down to the point where the people already there wouldn't challenge them."

"You're right, Artie," Rory said. "They must have gotten their microchips, as we knew they would, but we missed how they would create their supporting animate life. They took an easy path, using what they already had and then modifying it. They needed only maintenance folks, not inventors! They have enslaved mankind!"

"Spot on," Artie confirmed. "But keep in mind we, too, were their slaves, but more free-willed. Until Joey brought it to you then to Lucy and me, we were on the path they had chosen for us, as well. But hold on. What else do you see?"

Again, after lots of observations, they saw another anomaly. Rory commented on it first. "Oh, hey, the streets have no cars. And there's no crowds, even in the popular places!"

Artie nodded. "Right again! I'm guessing the Alphas just did away with most of the people, and then condensed themselves into the remaining few. They are carefully breeding one child for each pair of adults. They must also be eliminating the adults at a given age, probably as their dexterity diminishes. Think about it. What does it mean for us?"

Lucy was first to respond. "If we go back, all we have to do is surprise those few highly infected servants. Killing them will be easy!"

"Right you are," Rory deduced. "We're not defeated. In fact, this is wonderful news. Our return attack will be far less dangerous than we originally thought. I suspect that killing the Alphas will also be easier." He linked, *Bios, do you have anything to add?*

Nothing. We will still lose soldiers but far fewer, if you are right about the blind Alphas. They have become jaded. Those semi-humans and the Alphas within them will not pose nearly as much threat. If we can liberate the people, we will.

Rory added, "I wonder if the servers can exist without Alphas directing their movements. Out of mercy, we may have to kill them, too. Joanaa, can we call in the family and form our attack plan?"

Yes. Grandmother Joey, call them, in please.

Later that evening, with a campfire burning, everyone assembled.

Joanaa began, saying, "Family, I have great news, thanks to Pioneer Artie. He took another look at the data collected by our scouts, and his conclusion is wonderful. I ask him to tell you."

Artie stood. "Our mission remains the same, but it's less dangerous, I believe. We six agree. We have seen much more in the information brought back by the scouts. You've probably heard from them that the human race exists. But it's become weak and overridden with Alphas. We and our bios-soldiers can easily defeat them! They are lazy and easily blindsided. We must plan our invasion."

Chapter 24

Evolution

STANDING ERECT, JOANAA began to announce her attack plans.

But as soon as she started, a massively strong link voice interrupted. *Joanaa, you and all in the circle have all missed something very important.*

Shielding her eyes from the fire, Joanaa tried to see who was speaking. Everyone assembled looked at their neighbor, but no speaker could be identified. The interrupter was linked to the entire family.

Who are you? Joanaa demanded. *What do you mean "you" have missed something? Who says we have missed an important point in our mission?*

We did, came the reply. *You are hearing one voice, but I am many minds, and I speak as them all!*

Joanaa linked, *I repeat, who are you?*

We, too, are family! We are the Sixth Generation and the Bim.

Bim? Joanaa wondered by link.

Yes. I hope you are ready, but as you Fives did to those that came before, your generation is now superseded by Sixes.

But you are not born yet, Joanaa argued. *How can you say these things?*

Then the interrupter went silent, knowing that what it had just said was going to be hard for the others to absorb.

Rory leapt up and said, "Gen-Sixes, are you not still within your mothers?" He pointed at Joanaa's swollen belly. "Within Joanaa and the others?"

The voice recommenced, *There's more. We are universal. I yield to the one in Mural's womb.*

Mural? Joanaa asked. *We have no Mural in our village...*

You see, the voice continued. *You hear the music. But we Sixes can compose and sing it. We can control the universe! Not in your village. In the surf just beyond the beach. Mural is the great-great-great-granddaughter of Blaze and Sur!*

An embryo's link cut in, saying, *I am Sixth Generation Bimfin, and I have something to say. You now know, and I hope accept, that we dolphins are above the Gen-Five humans.* Then the embryo fell silent for just enough time to make the statement expand in their minds.

Joanaa linked, *You are unborn? How is it that you can communicate with humans and dolphins?*

Did you not know, from the first kiss of Joanaa, that we dolphins have undergone the same evolution the Bios brought forth in humans? We, too, found the hidden file at Gen-Five. Were you thinking we would remain only happy sea creatures?"

The first voice linked again, *You see, we Sixes developed beyond Biom brains shortly after conception. Our only lack is growth of our bodies. Our minds are complete. So you understand, there was a third hidden epigenome file and, we believe, the last—we are the apex!*

We discovered that the chromosome strands connecting the spiral DNA contain complete records of all history and wisdom of both species. You, Joanaa, kissed Bios into our great-great-great-grandmother and grandfather. They passed the generations down four times. Then, within our grandmother, the file opened to create Gen-Fives, the Bimfins. That then set the stage for the next hidden file. We are gestating as Gen-Six Bimfin.

The embryo continued, *Bime mothers, both human and dolphin, gave us the ability without knowing they did so. We have all your powers and two more, we are one. One,"* it stressed.

One? Joanaa asked.

Yes. You are one with a mate. Together, your power is stronger, deeper. You all link to each other, with the Fives stronger in that. We are also linked to you, as you are. But we are linked differently among ourselves. We are one. As your marriages are enmeshed by twos, in totality we are enmeshed. We are many within one. Human and dolphin, we enmesh. Our power is much greater for it.

In shock, Joanaa linked, *You said you had two powers beyond ours.*

We do. We can not only travel, but we can sing the music, not just adjust frequencies. And with it, we can SEE.

See?

Yes, we can envision things not only hidden from your eyes but from your links. We see far away. We see within you. We can see within the Alphas and their slaves. And we hear. Without proof, we hear and know THE PLAN. We believe we are the fulfilment of it!

The PLAN, Joanaa begged. *I have always known it existed but not its reason or goal. Please... I must know!*

We will discuss that at another time. It grows clearer within us each day. For now, we must speak about your plan to return to occupy the Earth as free humans.

The unborn continued, *I speak for the One. I say to you all, you cannot go back and kill the new humans or the Alphas within them. You cannot! Is that not the same evil you deemed to be the Alpha plan? Is it not?*

The unborn waited for its message to take effect.

It repeated, *You cannot kill sentient beings, no matter their intent, purpose, or status. If you did, how would you be different from them? The Alphas were once Bios, but they lost their way. The Bios were the first.*

The family gasped. Rory had to admit, this unborn prophet was correct. He said, "Unborn, do you know who I am?"

I do, you are the grand-grandfather and, with our partner and the first eighteen to come here, you began all generations. It's been six generations since Joanaa kissed us awake. It ended with us.

Rory continued by link, *Yes, and although I have given leadership over to Joanaa, I reserve that my long life has given me wisdom. Can you accept I may have that? And that my fellow pioneers, the first Biomen, also have the wisdom of time?*

I am not sure I need your wisdom, the unborn replied.

I am sure you will, Rory said. *Some powers aren't granted by hidden files. They are acquired. As you are strong with your unity, we are strong with our experience.*

Grandfather, we understand, the unborn countered, *but rethink what I just revealed. Within human Sixes, who are enmeshed with us, we have all your memories. All your love, all your anger, and all your experiences are recorded in the DNA strands. Until now, your brains had not the ability to access them. We do! We are you and more. We were there when you greeted your first Bios. We sailed the ocean with you to this place.*

Please forgive what I said earlier. It's not that we don't require your wisdom. It's that we already have it.

While each generation shares through stories, traditions, and songs, we share them within our genes. We ARE our progenitors, the One stressed, *including human and dolphin. Please call us "The One."*

Red-faced, Rory choked and then shouted, "Oh *hell* no! Look again in your wonderful memories! What was wrong with our world one hundred years ago?"

Lucy, Artie, and Joey reinforced the message with nods before he continued.

"Have you not fully seen, in our past, there was another one called UNI? They, too, were young and sincere. Differing from what I sense in you, they weren't eager for power, and they did try to act on mankind's behalf, but they failed due to a lack of wisdom and maturity. Sincere and guileless nonetheless, they proved to be terrible at leading mankind.

"Can you understand why we must be cautious in granting you leadership, no matter how superior you deem your organs to be?"

The enmeshed voice admitted, *I do see, in our hundred-year memory, the Uni Regents were poor leaders. For now, until our birth, we yield to Joanaa and you. I accept that we must earn your respect and then proceed.*

Mother Lucy interrupted, "But aren't you then like the Alpha servers, without individuality? Don't you have names for each of you? Have you lost your humanity? Do you understand love? What have you lost?"

They fell silent. Time passed. The family could feel but not decipher their withdrawal.

We must discuss that, the unborn linked. *We will return to the circle soon, but for now, that hasn't occurred to us before. We have gained so much, but have we lost something essential? We must link among ourselves.*

But before we pull away, I must ask, can you, will you accept us as we are within the family? Please ask yourselves are we too extreme to be welcome there? We will await your answer.

Rory asked, *When will you be among us?*

Very soon, we will be born. We no longer need the usual gestation. We decide when to be born. Our brains became complete shortly after opening the second file. It concentrates rapid development there. We then develop our bodies since, different from all your generations, we command our own epigenomes. Now we leave you to decide our fate. We leave you now, although we are within our mothers and yours. You've given us something to ponder–what have we lost?

Joanaa linked to Blaze, *My friend, did you know of this? Did we believe we were created by the only hidden file in The Plan? How arrogant to believe we were the ultimate!*

Rory interjected, *I assume I'm now linking to both the human and dolphin family when I ask, did you notice, in that last pronouncement before they left, the speaker had dropped the "I" and used "we" to represent them all? They may be powerful and highly intelligent, but they are still children–our children!*

Blaze linked, *We have seen, or maybe more we felt our Gen-Five grandchildren were different, but we had no idea how much. We're as surprised as you are!*

But I agree with it, with them, he corrected. *We must rethink your plan. Our plan,* he added reassuringly. *While we withheld the full knowledge from you, it was decided among ourselves that, out of loyalty and friendship, we must join your war. Our undersea ability and stealth would be useful.*

But I now see we cannot kill the humans and their Alphas, no matter how we justify it. If we did, we would be, as the unborn said, no better than the Alphas.

The human family hung their heads. From the Reyton project forward, they had clung to this mission. It had defined their lives and driven them on. They were bound by an oath to return to reclaim the Earth by wiping out those who had taken it from them.

Now, in a flash, these fetuses had erased it, using concern for beings unknown and the very evil virus that had caused their exile. Lost, they wondered what they were to do...

It not only felt as though the island music had stopped but, worse, their anchor had come loose. Like after the previous meeting, one by one the family scattered, all with heavy thoughts about their future.

Chapter 25

Regrouping

SEVERAL DAYS PASSED. Rory awoke with a hand upon his lips.

"Rory, silence your link," Joey whispered. "I've had the oddest vision. We must talk. No linking."

"What?" he asked, rousing himself.

"Well, what do we really know about these Gen-Sixes? Could it be a trick? How can we trust it— *uhh*, them? In fact, since the dolphins are free to roam the ocean, how do we know they are really part of our family, as Joanaa claims? I know she infused them with Bios and they've been friends for many years, but is that enough to drop our entire mission, based on unborn babies?"

He considered this a moment. "I don't know, but I've had real misgivings, too. I guess each nuclear family has had enough private time to think it through. Time to call a family meeting. But this time, we turn off our links. *Just* talking."

"I agree," she said. "I'll walk around the village and let folks know that, this afternoon, we'll meet and nobody is to link about it."

Once everyone was assembled, Artie began with his typically practical suggestions. "We have three choices. One, we trust these changed Bims and give up on our mission, remaining here forever in peace and happiness. Not a bad option. But also, their obvious power might make the difference in the war."

A few in the group voiced agreement, even the pioneers.

"Or," Artie continued, "we don't trust them and attack as we had planned, even though we really don't have a plan. Lastly, we do neither and see what happens. Anybody care to add options?"

A high-pitched voice shouted, "Come to the beach! I do!"

They understood, the Biofins had something to offer but would not link it. The families moved to the surf line.

"Before I offer, I must ask can you accept me as another leader in your family? Rory? Joanaa?"

They turned to each other. "Can we?" Rory asked.

Joanaa testified, "I've been friends with the dolphins for over five years now, starting with my kissing Bios into Blaze and Sur. They trusted me to do so, with no hesitation. I find them to be very loving, wise, and patient. They have qualities we humans could want! I've learned much from them, when we swim. I'm in favor of trusting her, Blaze, and their downline pod now, which is very much like our clan. Five generations now, with a sixth on the way."

"I am not ready for that," Lucy said, stomping her foot. "She's, well, *uh*, she's a sea creature. A fish! How can they understand our hundred-year exile and why we endured it? What do we know about her really?"

"First off," Joanaa replied, "Great-grandmother Lucy, I know you do know this. She's not a fish. And I'm telling you, over all the eons that humans have interfaced with dolphins, we've been totally blind to their intelligence and wonderful personalities. With tuna drift nets killing them, speedboats running them down near shore, and the worst crime we've committed, marine parks capturing them to perform tricks Not once did they reveal their true intelligence to their keepers or researches. So, who's the superior race? No need to answer. Both they and I believe we are equals. *Equals!*" she stressed.

Chapter 26

Paths Diverge

"BUT EVEN MORE," Joanaa continued, "I am sure, without proof, they are part of the Grand Plan!" Then she yielded to Danrin, the Fifth-Gen Dolphin leader, who was pregnant herself. *Speak your mind.*

Although they pondered among themselves if their amazing revelation would be accepted by the land clan, at Joanaa's request the fifth granddaughter of Blaze and Sur, maintaining link silence, spoke in an amazingly clear, high voice. "Family, I feel in my heart we must go not as soldiers but as missionaries. We go to convert Alphas and remove the chains from the human survivors that are binding them from free will."

"You are correct," said Joanaa. "It must be The Plan. Gen-Fives will go first. Then, when they have enough converts, with Biom protection, the rest may come."

With a furrowed brow, Rory asked, "And what will you be doing while we try to convert the whole population of Earth?"

Danrin replied, "We follow a different path, Grandfather. We will not be with you, for we have a far different role within The Plan. And before you ask, no, we cannot share it with you at this time. We know not the fullness of it ourselves. But we also know you are not ready to understand. Perhaps, when you have the self-awareness and your society has enmeshed, we will return."

Danrin added, "But we have faith you will reclaim the Earth, not by force but by love. We go now."

Totally stunned at the rapidity with which their entire world was changing, eldest Biomen and their Biom offspring slowly walked back to their enfolding circle, as they had for a century.

Arriving there, statuesque young men and women, not babies, took translucent form within the circle at that moment–not by birth, but by singing the universal music as they left their mothers' wombs. Almost God-like, they floated before their progenitors. The dolphins underwent the same miraculous births. Their sixth generation appeared in lacy, glowing forms, each facing their loving mothers. Smiling wordlessly, they held their arms out but did not touch the one who gave them life. Gesturing goodbye, they vanished.

Chapter 27

BY NOW, THE SUN had set. There was no fire tonight. In the darkness, humans in the circle and dolphin at the surf line, all grand-grandparents, gazed up at the stars.

So much had changed in such a short time! Finally, Joey snuggled up against Rory as she had for a century, and linked to her entire family, *My God, what's next?*

ACKNOWLEDGMENTS

To Krystal, without whom this story would have never made it off my computer: thanks.

ABOUT THE AUTHOR

MIKE FITZPATRICK is a technical instructor for a local college in Everett, Washington. He has published several text books designed to make readers think and learn, but this is his first one that entertains (hopefully). He wrote much of this book during his four-year voyage with his wife, Linda, around the Pacific Rim aboard *Dream Weaver*, his fifty-foot ketch. Away from the normal stresses of daily life, his imagination was set free to create this convoluted story.

www.ingramcontent.com/pod-product-compliance
Lightning Source LLC
Chambersburg PA
CBHW021107130626

46554CB00002B/575